PICKING UP JELLYFISH

To Kay -
watch out
for jellyfish -
Best wishes,
Ray Oliver
4-3-08

PICKING UP JELLYFISH

Or: The Bobble Head Legacy

A Novel

Ray Oliver

iUniverse, Inc.
New York Lincoln Shanghai

Picking Up Jellyfish
Or: The Bobble Head Legacy

Copyright © 2007 by Ray Oliver

iUniverse books may be ordered through booksellers or by contacting:

iUniverse
2021 Pine Lake Road, Suite 100
Lincoln, NE 68512
www.iuniverse.com
1-800-Authors (1-800-288-4677)

ISBN: 978-0-595-43110-6 (pbk)
ISBN: 978-0-595-68205-8 (cloth)
ISBN: 978-0-595-87452-1 (ebk)

Printed in the United States of America

To Cindy—wife, mother, lover,
friend, and typist.

BEFORE

CHAPTER 1

A Midwinter Day's Awakening

Or: Accentuate the Accent

It all began with a dream. I was being seduced by Julianne Moore. She was singing about me being her love machine, and yelling for me to take her, to make her my love slave. Then the alarm started ringing, causing the love machine to go on the fritz, causing me to wonder what the hell a fritz is, and how I ended up on one.

I was not pleased, especially since it was early Saturday morning. My wife, the one who had forgotten to unset the alarm, groggily turned it off. Within two minutes, her sleep breaths told me that she had returned to whatever dream she might have been enjoying. Probably the George Clooney dream. I turned, and then considered tossing. Unlike most people, who toss and then turn, I always turn first. Since I had nothing in my hand, I skipped the tossing altogether. I lie motionless, sleepless, Julianneless. I could have said Mooreless, but using the first name was more intimate. I like it, more or less.

That's when I decided to write a book. It seemed like everyone else had written one: celebrities, almost celebrities, politicians, criminals. I know these things, since I work in a bookstore. I decided that I would write a romantic novel.

I know, it's not like the world is clamoring for another romantic novel. But mine would be different. How many 43-year-old male romantic novelists are there? I'd start with the cover. I'd put real people on it, people with wrinkles or receding hairlines or beer bellies. Okay, maybe that's not such a good idea. The cover should attract people, make them want to pick it up, not actively avoid it. Maybe I could find the female Fabio alternative. Maybe Julianne would pose for the cover. Maybe in my dreams.

Maybe a romance novel isn't such a great idea. I'm not exactly Jude Law. I'm more like common law. And who wants to spend all day writing about heaving breasts and burning loins, especially when burning loins sounds like a serious medical problem, or a rock band. Can't you just hear the radio announcer, in his best used-car salesman's voice, screaming, "Coming soon, to a city near you, it's the Burning Loin tour, with special opening act Anal Floss." I think anal floss is the new, hip term for a thong, but I'm not sure. "New" and "hip" are words not usually used around me. Which is kind of unfair, because I have the youngest mind I know.

I contemplated other genres. I like the word contemplate for some reason. It's sexy for thinking. I contemplated political thrillers, but that sounded like an oxymoron. I thought about detective stories, murder and suspense and fantasy and science fiction. I wanted to write the Great American Novel (hereafter, the G.A.N.). I wanted to make a difference.

After two hours of turning and contemplating, I woke up my wife and we made semi-passionate love. That's not a criticism. We were just short on heaving breasts and burning loins. I guess that's because of the prelude to foreplay, or fore foreplay if you will, that more mature lovers go through. I woke her gently, rubbing her back and nibbling her ear. She didn't object. Don't tell me those Julianne Moore/George Clooney dreams aren't helpful. But unlike the movies, my wife's first words were, "Okay, but first I have to pee." It's so romantic. Of course, the minute she got up to use the bathroom I had to pee. My wife took her time, adding washing and teeth brushing to the routine. She climbed back in bed as I left to repeat the process. I was not about to be out-peed, out-washed, or out-brushed.

When we were both finally in the same bed at the same time, spontaneity shot all to hell, we had to start from scratch, which is a terrible term, especially in this case. What was ever accomplished "from scratch?" It sure wouldn't help if I scratched her now—unless you count gentle back scratching, but that wasn't my modus operandi. I like those two words, they sound sensual. "Hey baby, you want to modus operandi?"

"Not tonight, I have a headache."

So we made semi-passionate love. Not slam-bam love, but not fireworks and violin love either. Pedestrian love. Not like we were walking around or anything. We aren't contortionist. It was pedestrian in the sense of ordinary, comfortable, safe. There is a lot to be said for pedestrian love.

After we were done, I started to tell her about my dream, but she stopped me. My wife, Jessica, is the smartest person I know. She said, "Adam, a little fantasy and a few secrets are healthy. I don't need the bloody details." I love it when my tall, slender, brown-eyed Southern belle uses British slang. I have no idea why she does it, or why it pleases me, but it does.

Ours is a mixed marriage. Jessica was born in Biloxi, Mississippi, moved to Nashville, Tennessee when she was nine, and graduated from the University of Tennessee. I was born in Salem, Massachusetts, home of the Puritans and the witchcraft trials. I'm a UMass grad who met his wife in Washington D.C. while celebrating Earth Day. In addition to the geographical mixture, there is the religious integration. She was raised by Southern Baptists; I was indoctrinated by Roman Catholics. Her parents were not happy. Until the day they died, they almost never said a bad word to my face, but I could tell they were disappointed she had chosen a bloody Catholic. A Yankee Catholic no less. We got married in her parents' church, and that was the last time we set foot in it, until their funerals.

My parents were worse. Until the day they died, they treated Jessica like she was the anti-Christ, or a least the anti-Pope, which is why we saw them as little as possible. Even though I have never forgiven my parents for that, I somehow find myself missing them, which really ticks me off, but I do. How can you miss mean, narrow-minded people? Why should you still want parental approval, after all these years, even when they are gone?

Every time we buried a parent, Jessica and I grew closer. It's a pain we shared, becoming orphans. For the first few years we heard a lot of concern about which church the children would attend. Then we heard a lot about whether we were ever going to have children. We never told them the truth; that we tried and failed, that neither of us were capable of baby production. By the time the expense and the technology made artificial means at least feasible, we felt that we were too old. I think Jessica is the extraordinary kindergarten teacher she is today because of this. Every year she has twenty-some children, all hers for a year. Every summer begins with a postpartum depression. I think all four parents went to their graves resenting us for denying them grandchildren. They certainly weren't grand parents, so I doubt if they would have been decent grandparents. We'll never know.

Our parents could never get past the accents. One night, Jessica's father, in a rare moment of bourbon-induced candor, declared, "I swear, I can't never understand hardly a word all you Yankees say. It sure is aggravatin.'" I didn't know what to say, so I said nothing, just sat there with this fake smile, nodding like a bobble head and hoping he'd change the subject. He didn't.

"What, you find that funny or sumpin'?"

"Not really, no, I don't."

"Then why you got that shit-eatin' grin?"

I resisted the temptation to comment on his descriptive prowess, but I couldn't resist being a smartass, since it was sort of in keeping with the flow of the conversation. "I'm sorry, I was just thinking how sad that must be for you."

"Sad? What in the blue blazes are you talking about?"

I had no idea where the blue blazes was, or were if there were several of them, so, in my best, golly gee whilickers voice, I replied, "Yes, sad. I mean, you can't listen to the national news, or watch most movies, or sporting events, or anything." I saw that I'd hit a nerve, and I should have been smart enough or decent enough to shut up. That's when I added, "I never knew how hard it is," I paused here, perfecting my timing, before adding, "for y'all."

If the look on his face didn't tell me I'd gone too far, and it did, the look on Jessica's reinforced it. The difference was that, hours later, okay, days later, Jessica was able to find the humor in it. I had learned to say "y'all" the correct way, not like some good ol' boy wanna be, who goes around saying, "you all." Jessica's father never did see the humor in it. I apologized, not that it did any good.

My mother was worse. She could not be more Bostonian in her speech. One day, with Jessica standing beside me, she asked, "Why, in the name of Heaven, do they all have to use that Gawd awful accent?" I knew two things. One, whenever my mother started using "they" or "them" it was always derogatory, pejorative, or hurtful. It usually involved some sort of stereotype. The second thing I knew was that things could be awful, or they could be Gawd awful. Apparently, my wife's accent fell into the latter category. The third thing I knew (yes, I know I said there were only two, but when I get rolling I'm not always in control) was that I was about to enter a stupid conversation with a woman who had the tact of Godzilla.

"Mom, is it possible that you are the one with the accent?"

If I had burped and farted in the middle of communion, she would not have worn a more pained expression. She stared, as if trying to first recognize, and then castrate, the offending Visigoth. "No, I don't think so."

"Well, to people in the South you do."

Clearly, she was searching her mind for the cause of her parental failings. Through gritted teeth, she managed, "We are not in the South, thank you very much, and I'd appreciate not being contradicted about this. They don't speak English." Then, with a quick look at Jessica, she added, "No offense, dear."

I told here there was offense taken, and stormed out of the room, only to storm back in yelling, "The whole world laughs when you pahk your cah at Harvahd yahd." Then I stormed out again. This time Jessica saw the humor first. Maybe the parental crabgrass is always greener at the other family's house. My mother just didn't understand what all the fuss was about, but certainly didn't mean to cause a scene. That was as close as she ever came to saying she was sorry. I'm not sure she ever said those words. I guess when you're always right, at least in you own miniscule mind, you don't have to be sorry.

The whole thing left a pessimistic taste in my mouth—a taste foreign to someone often labeled a cock-eyed optimist. I hate that term. Even ignoring the obvious, cheap sexual illusion, it's a stupid phrase. I want to be a straight-eyed optimist, but it's difficult. How can we hope to overcome racial, sexual, religious, or ethnic divides, when two white Anglo-Saxon families can't get past accents and geography?

"Gawd awful" did become part of our vocabulary. We've had many a cheap laugh using those two words. We've eaten Gawd awful food, gone to Gawd awful movies, heard Gawd awful music. We've even lived through a few Gawd awful presidents.

That's why I've got to write the Great American Novel (hereafter, the G.A.N.). Cue the inspirational music. I want to tilt at windmills, educate and inspire the masses, and move mythic mountains. But most of all, I want to rid the world of its Gawd awfulness.

CHAPTER 2

Bush League

Or: Memory Lane

History and sexual escapades often repeat themselves, but not always. The next morning, I awoke without the alarm. There was no Julianne Moore, either. A quick turn, a little contemplation, and there was only one thing left to do—try for a repeat performance. The love of my life responded with a groan, a less than happy, totally unsexual groan. Then she added a less than amorous, "Go back to sleep." She did. I didn't. Instead, I got up and indulged in one of life's greatest pleasures (although not as great as my initial idea). It was time for coffee and the Sunday paper.

It was slightly above freezing when I went outside to get the paper. I made a slight detour, going to the backyard kennel to fetch our child substitute, Atticus. Atticus is the friendliest golden retriever known to man. He is named after the greatest of all literary heroes, Atticus Finch. I fed him, let him romp around our five-acre woods while I retrieved the paper, then the two of us went inside. Atticus helped me build a fire in our fieldstone fireplace, if by help one means he kept nudging my hand and crowding against me so that I wouldn't forget him. I drank my coffee, and for the next two hours I read the paper, occasionally petting my companion as he stretched out by my chair, basking in the warmth of the crackling logs until he fell asleep. I was on the verge myself, but an event from my past started to weave its ugly memory yet again into my consciousness.

I was twelve years old. I was a catcher on the all-star little league team, try-ing to win our way to the mecca of all big league dreamers—Williamsport, Pennsylvania and the Little League World Series. It was the last inning, and we had a two to one lead. There were two outs and two on when Ricky Razzoni came to the plate. Ricky was, by far, their best hitter. He was also my friend.

Ricky had gotten a hit every time up. The last time, our coach, Coach Mel-horne, went absolutely ballistic at our starting pitcher, who just happened to be his son, Darren. Coach Melhorne honestly thought we were the Yankees, and he was Ralph Houk. In the dugout, he had a "conference" with Darren and me. He said, "Next time, we brush him back. I don't care if you hit him, he's not going to hit us again."

Darren was a good kid, and he could have been a good pitcher if he had bet-ter control (or a different coach). His father never let up. He was the epitome of the frustrated athlete vicariously reliving his glory through his son. He was intense, with a comment about everything. He barked orders between every pitch, Darren getting more uptight the more he barked. I honestly expected to hear him yell, "Inhale, Darren. Good. Now exhale. Look for the signal. Inhale again. Get ready. Exhale. Come on son, relax."

Relax? I was a nervous wreck, and I wasn't the one being yelled at. Anyway, Ricky comes up and I see Darren glance at his father, who nods his head as if reminding him to brush him back. It didn't occur to me then that it takes a real idiot to coach this way. Ricky stands in and the first pitch comes inside, about belt high and Ricky jumps back and takes ball one. I glance over at our coach, and he's smiling. He motions for Darren to do it again, and as I throw the ball back to our pitcher I whisper for Ricky to be alert, but I'm not sure he gets it. I never caught the next pitch. This time, the brush back is behind Ricky's head, but his first instinct is to move backwards, away from the plate. He tried to duck as he moved back, but it was too late. The ball caught him square in the face, somehow missing the batting helmet but not missing his nose and mouth. It made a sharp yet soggy sound, like a wet towel being snapped against a wooden door. Ricky never said a word, just crumpled to the ground, where he lie motionless. One of the parents was a doctor, who immediately rushed to my friend's aid. It was my first encounter with blood, and fear. I wanted to vomit, but I didn't. I wanted to cry, but I didn't. I wanted to tell Coach Melhorne that he was an asshole, but I didn't. Instead, I watched as the doctor did his best to stop the bleeding. By the time the ambulance arrived, Ricky was a scared, pathetic-looking kid with a broken nose and a fat lip and a rapidly closing left eye. After Ricky was rushed away, the unthinkable happened. We finished the game. With the based loaded and two outs, the next petrified hitter struck out on three pitches. It is not easy to hit a ball when you are bailing out because you are afraid.

When the third out was made, Coach Melhorne jumped out of the dugout, clapping and cheering as if his son had just won the seventh game of the World Series. The rest of us didn't share his enthusiasm, especially Darren, who looked like he was in the last hour of a 48-hour flu. We never made it to Williamsport; in fact, we lost the next game.

Three decades later, I remember that sound, and Ricky's face, and Melhorne's callousness. I visited Ricky daily. We warmed the bench together on our high school baseball team. Ricky never once showed the slightest fear when he resumed playing ball, but he never seemed able to hit after the incident. Darren got cut from the team. He peeked at twelve, and his father could no longer control his future.

After Jessica and I got married, I volunteered to coach a little league team. I was determined to be everything Coach Melhorne was not—fair, caring, and a good teacher. I enjoyed the kids, and I'd like to think they learned something while having fun. But I hated the experience. Macho men and belligerent women; win at all cost coaches and obnoxious parents ruined the game for me, and their kids. It wasn't fun, wasn't even a game. After three years of coaching, I'd had all the yelling and arguing and selfishness I could stand. I will always love the game of baseball. I will always hate the parents who abuse it.

Atticus had just gotten up and stretched when Jessica joined us. Of course, this set his twenty horsepower tail into overdrive as be bounced to greet her. For two minutes they let each other know how wonderful it was to see each other. It is possible that I may have mentioned, for the umpteenth time, what a wonderful world it would be if people were as demonstrative as dogs. It is possible that, for the umpteenth time, I made some disgustingly chauvinistic remark about tail wagging when I entered the room. It is possible that, for the umpteenth time, my wife rolled her eyes and suggested I do something that is anatomically impossible. I do know that umpteenth is bigger than a bunch, but smaller than a gazillion, and that I hate it when I am predictable.

When Atticus had settled down, my wife began her Sunday ritual, which consisted of doing the New York Times crossword puzzle in ink. Nobody likes a show off. A short time later I put my dog back in his kennel, ignoring his, "you can't be serious, how dare you be so cruel when you know I'd never do this to you" eyes. I went back inside, turned on a basketball game, and promptly fell asleep. Sometimes remembering wears me out.

CHAPTER 3

Muddy Waters

Or: The Good, the Bad, and the Muddy

Rainy days and Mondays almost never get me down. I like my job, at least most of it, and I don't mind the rain. The day after a rainy day contains that crystalline quality that makes the whole world feel like fresh-washed jeans. But to get that fresh-washed feeling, you have to do the washing, just like you can't get to Friday without passing through Monday. It all comes out in the wash, so to speak, and I've learned to go with the flow, roll with the tide and the punches, and any other cliché that applies.

On this particular rainy Monday, I was driving my Toyota pickup toward the large bookstore/coffee shop that I manage. It's one of those mammoth, corporate chains that I swore I'd never be a part of. Don't get me started on how many times I've compromised on that kind of thing. I like the word "compromise." It's so much kinder than sold out, or wimped out.

It was early in the morning, allowing me the opportunity to easily navigate what would later become a gauntlet, an obstacle course of strip malls and fast food and car dealerships known as Kingston Pike. At certain times it was a bumper-to-bumper parking lot, a fitting tribute to, actually, I have no idea what it is a fitting tribute to. I just know I hate doing the Kingston crawl, so I always beat the morning rush hour traffic. It's good for my sanity, and it allows me to ease into my workday.

There was an S.U.V. stopped at the red light as I neared my place of employment. As I approached, I watched the driver's side window go down, the driver's hand reached out, and a McDonald's™ bag, coffee cup, and various wrappers hit the pavement. Just then, the light turned green and the vehicle sped off, as if the driver had practiced and perfected this kind of escape. My headlights seemed to catch the two stickers affixed to his bumper, rather than his license plate. The first sticker read **DUCKS UNLIMITED**. The second read **SUPPORT OUR TROOPS**. Perfectly centered on the hatchback above them was the omnipresent (at least in the South) fish—the religious fish. There was too much irony, too much hypocrisy, and too much trash. It never fails to disgust me, but it no longer surprises me. If it hadn't been raining, I might have picked up the trash. Don't laugh. I've done that kind of thing before.

It was after ten before my next highlight occurred. I define a highlight as something I can laugh about, or bitch about, when Jessica and I sit down at the end of the day and compare notes. Not that either of us has anything written. It's just another stupid phrase.

Our bookstore has a large bulletin board. People are constantly coming in to put up fliers on the board. Of course, they're not really fliers because they tend to stay put, but anyway, people use our board to advertise all types of merchandise and coming attractions (as opposed to going attractions). The highlight of my day came when a five-foot tall, four-foot wide woman waddled into our store and asked permission to post her poster about an upcoming mud-wrestling event. I must admit, I was taken aback, or a front, or sideways, because, without thinking (again), I semi-shrieked, "Mud-wrestling? People still do that?" The voice screeched and cracked like puberty revisited, or maybe reverse puberty. Immediately I knew I had been insensitive. I knew before she replied, "Yes, and you don't have to be so insensitive."

I apologized profusely, and was semi-successful at making her relax. I discovered that she was helping to raise money for the homeless shelter, which made me feel even dumber. Then she asked if I'd like to go, and because of the guilt from my original outburst, I found myself in possession of two tickets to a Saturday night mud-wrestling extravaganza.

Jessica not only saw the humor in it, she insisted that we attend, and five nights later, we did. Yee Haw! The crowd was worth the price of admission. I had often wondered what kind of person would go to one of these events. Now I knew. I was that kind of person. I wonder if I'm scarred for life.

Jessica did not stop laughing the entire evening, so I guess it was worth it. She said the action was Gawd awful, and I told her I might use it in the Great American Novel (hereafter, the G.A.N.) America. Land of the free, home of the muddy.

CHAPTER 4

Jellyfish

Or: Life in the Dark

I may have been six. Or seven. I suppose I could have been eight, I really don't remember. All I know for sure is that I was at the beach with some friend's family. I know I wasn't with my family because they hated the sun, the water, and the Gawd awful sand that, "Just gets into everything."

So we were wading, splashing, bouncing in the waves. My friend had gone in to dry off, and I was about to follow when I was captivated by this colorful, pulsating life blob that came floating by. I had never seen anything like it, and my cat-killing curiosity got the better of me. I touched it, first with a finger, then with my entire hand. I wanted to pick it up, to examine the long tendrils that were dangling beneath it, even though I was too young to know what a tendril was at the time.

I remember that my first sensation was one of surprise at the Jell-o-like™ texture. I remember the tingling, stinging sensation that made me drop this curiosity, and I remember wondering what was causing my discomfort. I guess I didn't make the connection, because I tried to examine it again. I know how dumb that sounds now, but that's what I did. After the second time I grabbed it, I did make the connection, because it felt like twenty bees were attacking my arm. I was sore from my fingers to my elbow, and I remember running to my friend's mother with tears running down my cheeks and fear growing in my heart.

What I remember most, other than the pain of a hundred bumped funny bones, which by the way is not the least bit funny, was the feeling of being in the dark. It was like every person on that beach, maybe every person in the whole world knew that you shouldn't pick up a jellyfish. I alone didn't know. Was there a memo sent out? A lesson in school that I had missed? A warning, like the one on my mattress, that I had ignored or discarded at penalty of death? How come I hadn't gotten this message?

My friend's mom used ice and the omni-present elixir of my childhood, Bactine™, to soothe my physical hurt. Only time really helped. It would take longer to soothe the psychological damage. Sometimes I think it is ongoing. That feeling of being in the middle of a private joke that everyone gets except you continues to haunt me. Nothing angers me more than being the last to know.

Thanks to dear old mom and dad, I had that feeling about sex. I had that feeling all through high school and most of college when it came to political and religious and musical discussions. That's why I became a reader, a traveler, an activist. I would not be the last to know, not if I could help it.

Thinking back on that day, I learned that being sheltered is not the same as being protected. I learned that curiosity is a good thing, even though there are times when we get hurt by it. I learned that life is about contradictions, and that I'm still learning how to deal with them. I'm learning that I want to be bold yet safe, daring yet secure.

It was more than twenty years later that I began thinking about that day. I found the humor in my inability to connect the stinging sensation with the jellyfish. When I told Jessica about it, she laughed as I exaggerated my, "Duh, let's see if it stings again" mentality. For a while, it became a metaphor, or a cliché, for every silly or thoughtless act I committed. Jessica took great pleasure in saying, "Adam Donahue, you are picking up a bloody jellyfish again." Occasionally, she still does.

I've learned to laugh about it. I've reached the point where I'm glad it happened. It's a wonderful reminder that sometimes we all pick up jellyfish, and sometimes we get hurt, but life goes on and pain subsides and lessons are learned. And being kept in the dark is worse than finding things out the hard way, no matter how much it hurts.

CHAPTER 5

Not So Crystal Clear

Or: Fire

Nothing is prettier than spring in the South. For fall foliage, I'll take New England, but for that cosmic transition from winter's chill to summer's warmth, pear trees and daffodils and dogwoods and redbuds and fragrant wildflowers too numerous to name make the South the king of spring.

It was a glorious spring day when a most inglorious event occurred, an event that would change my life forever.

Jessica had arrived home from school while Atticus and I were romping in the woods. I hadn't heard her arrive. It was only after I'd brushed my dog and filled his water dish that I noticed her car. I was surprised she hadn't joined us, as was her custom. It was only after I'd put Atticus in the kennel and went inside that I discovered why.

I was greeted by sight I had never seen before. The love of my life was sitting at the kitchen table, staring into space, tears rolling down her cheeks. She had not heard me enter, literally jumping at my, "What's wrong?" intrusion on her painful reverie. She looked at me blankly, like I was a stranger, before blinking herself back to reality.

I repeated the question, waiting as the most articulate woman I knew struggled to find the illusive words. "Do you remember Donna Jo Crawford?"

I had never met Donna Jo, but I had received almost daily briefings about this loving child who was so desperate for attention and affection. It was mandatory, almost like a law or a commandment, that my wife had at least one student who broke her heart every year. Usually, it was a student who had great potential but little hope for a healthy childhood because of his or her home situation. This year, it was Donna Jo. She was the one whose parents never attended any school function. She was the one with the radiant smile and the filthy clothes. She was the one who didn't look forward to the weekends, who had nothing to show or to tell, who clung to her teacher a little tighter each day. As those thoughts raced through my head, I found myself nodding in answer to my wife's question, waiting for her to continue.

"Donna Jo is in the hospital. She's got burns ..." My wife stopped. She wasn't exactly crying, and she wasn't exactly shaking, and she wasn't exactly drifting into some altered state or place, but she was unable to continue.

It was a long night. Through stops and starts and involuntary shudders and sighs, I was finally able to understand what had rocked Jessica's soul. I was to learn about meth, crystal meth, methamphetamine. At first, I couldn't understand what drugs had to do with a kindergarten student, but my wife is a good teacher. I learned that meth is running rampant in Tennessee. I learned that its list of "ingredients" could include Sudafed™ and Drano™, air-conditioning Freon™, cough syrup, or any gross and flammable material that can be cooked or boiled into a toxic mess that can later be smoked or snorted or injected.

Donna Jo Crawford was the only daughter of a mother and father who used and abused and sold meth. In fact, that was their primary source of income. It seems that last evening Donna Jo's mother and father were cooking meth, like it was a steak or something. It also seems that, while they were cooking, they were sampling their products. All the while, sweet, innocent Donna Jo slept in her small bedroom in the back of the house.

The police weren't sure if the parents passed out or had gotten careless and forgetful, but they were convinced that some cooking was left unattended for a long time; long enough for there to be an explosion. The father was closest to the stove. He probably died instantly. The mother was still alive, but her prognosis was not good. Donna Jo's bedroom caught on fire. The plucky little girl got out a window, but her clothes and hair were burning. By the time she remembered to "stop, drop, and roll," she had suffered varying degrees of burns. She and her mother were flown to the University of Tennessee Medical Center. The mother remained unconscious, but Jessica had somehow learned that Donna Jo continued to cry out during the flight. Here words were, "I'm sorry, I'll try harder, I'll be good." Over and over, like a litany or a chant, "I'm sorry, I'll try harder, I'll be good."

I never asked my wife how she learned this. I only knew that if she repeated it she had every reason to believe it, and I accepted it without question.

Long into the night we talked about Donna Jo's parents. We talked about the kind of people who expose their child to the pollution of a deadly chemical concoction. We talked about the pain and the fear a young child must feel upon awakening to a conflagration, an inferno fit for hell.

If someone were to ever ask me what I like best about my wife, I would answer, "her heart." No one is more loving. No one cares so deeply. I was beginning to realize that her greatest strength might, on this particular evening, become her greatest weakness. She could not hold or comfort Donna Jo. She, who could not have children of her own, had to watch helplessly as those who could, destroyed theirs. Her heart was breaking, and I was powerless to stop it.

CHAPTER 6

Movement

Or: Bobble Head Ping-Pong

For three days, Donna Jo lapsed in and out of consciousness. For three days, my wife taught school, then left for the hospital. On the second day I joined her. I could only imagine the student my wife had known. The one I saw was black and purple and blistered in the few areas that were still visible. Most of her body was an avalanche of gauze. I found myself fixating on her lips. I remembered how often my wife had talked about her smile. Smiling, in fact any movement now, would be painful if it were still possible. I imagined them moving, smiling, talking to her teacher. Then I imagined them mumbling, "I'm sorry, I'll try harder, I'll be good." I learned that it is possible to hate someone you had never met. I hated Donna Jo's mother and her dead father.

On the third day, my wife returned from the hospital visibly upset. "They're flying her to Cincinnati—to the Shriners Hospital. They have a better burn unit." It was an obvious setback. It was the first time I thought about the possibility of this ending in death. I worried about what it would do to my wife, who was shaking her head and clinching her fists as she observed, "I won't be able to see her now. And if I don't, no one will. She will lie in a hospital bed with no visitors, no one to tell her that they love her, that she'll get better. She'll be afraid, and alone, and, she just might give up."

Jessica believed in the importance of the mind in the healing process. So did I. She believed that Donna Jo would be helped by hearing her voice, even if she couldn't respond. So did I. She believed Shriners Hospital was the best place for her, yet she grieved for the loss the separation would create. So did I. Cincinnati was four hours away.

I knew that Jessica would have gone to Cincinnati if she didn't have her other students to worry about. They were struggling with what happened to their classmate, and they needed their teacher. Faced with incredible pain and pressure, my wife had to teach and guide and console twenty-five other kindergarteners. I wondered why our society continued to underpay and under appreciate people like my wife. I wondered why I make more money while she touched move lives. I wondered when we would go to Cincinnati. I actually knew the answer long before the next weekend, the one Jessica selected for our trip.

The ride to the Ohio city was almost normal, like old times. After an hour of semi-silent driving, Jessica looked at me and asked, "Are door nails deader than other nails?" It was a challenge.

We used to travel frequently, especially when our parents were alive. We often sat, like bobble heads, keeping time to the music, or nodding along as one of us pontificated about some personal or social issue. Jessica created the verbal game that I dubbed bobble head ping-pong because, well, it was like two bobble heads firing verbal volleys back and forth. Either party could serve. The serve was some random quote or question or cliché. The only requirement was that an equally random response had to follow quickly. Both of us accused the other of preparing mental lists to use, a "planned spontaneity" of sorts. Of course the accusations were correct. It had been some time since we had played, but I was not about to falter once the challenge had been issued.

"What was the first straw?"

Jessica smiled for the first time in days before returning, "How cute is a button?" The game was on.

"How cool are cucumbers?"

"That's a foul, you've used that before." Both of us tended to makeup rules as we went along.

"There's never been a rule against repetition. I think you're stalling for time."

"There should be a rule against it, since it shows no creativity. Originality should count for something."

I was hurt, wounded, cut to the quick, whatever the hell that is, although I knew she was right. "Fine. Scratch the cucumber. How pretty is a penny?"

"That's better. How quiet is a mouse?"

My wife wasn't only answering, she was providing commentary—almost like bobble head trash talking. "If a girl is staying in a halfway house and she goes all the way, well, how does that add up? Do you smoke half a cigarette afterwards?"

Jessica's eyes widened, her mouth widened, ever her nostrils widened. "First of all, WHAT? How does that follow? And secondly, that's two questions. That's ridiculous, although mildly amusing."

"It's only a slight variation, a backhand instead of a forehand. You starting with silly questions, I just went in a different, less clichéd area. I'm willing to drop the second question, but you have got to do better that 'mildly amusing.' I want freakin' funny at the very least. And you need to play or admit defeat."

"Fine. It was freakin' funny. So my question is, 'How funny is freakin' funny?"

"That's better. If Saturday Night Live is a rerun, who do they still call it Saturday Night Live?"

"Why do people, mainly guys, always talk about taking a leak? Shouldn't they leave a leak?"

"I thought you didn't like double questions. Have you ever rested in a restroom?"

"Has your blood ever boiled?"

We were getting into a rhythm, freely associating nonsensical, non-sequiturial ramblings when, in an obviously thoughtless moment, I asked, "Are there live deadbeat dads?"

The game was over. Once again, I found myself craving a verbal eraser. I was an immature child taking a joke too far, carelessly blurting out something that had no business being blurted out. We were traveling to Cincinnati to visit the victim of a man who was a deadbeat when he was alive. Now that he was dead, and his wife and daughter in danger of dying, I could not have managed a more inappropriate reminder of our mission. The game was supposed to be about fun, escape, innocence. I immediately said all of the things people say when they feel the shame of an un-clever remark wash over them. There was the awkward pause, the rapid-fire explanation/apology/rationalization. Then there was more awkward silence. My wife was able to force that semi, "this isn't really funny but I'll smile anyway," sort of smile, and later she was able to add, "My husband keeps picking up jellyfish." When I pointed out that I only did it once, this time, she smiled what I hoped was a more genuine smile. Then we rode in silence.

The thing about silence is knowing when to break it. I never know. I drove, wanting to say so many things and daring to say none. I was on the verge of playing some music, an act that would have ended the silence but driven us deeper into our own thoughts. Jessica let me off the hook. "Ya know why meth is so popular in our area?"

I was relieved to have a reason to speak. "Because it's cheap to make?"

"Yes. Partially. Also because we have so much land, and so little population."

"I'm not sure I'm following."

"It's hard to cook up meth in an apartment complex. Too many people would smell it. But out in the country, away from everyone else, it's easy to create your own lab. That's how it started."

"Didn't Donna Jo live in a subdivision?"

"Yes. A poor one, to be sure. That's the problem. It's spreading to more populated areas."

I wasn't sure how to respond. Everyone grieves differently. My wife's way of dealing with grief was to read, to study, and to educate herself. It was like she withdrew into books. Now, she was sharing that information with me. "So Donna Jo's neighbors were at risk?"

"Absolutely. It's a miracle that no other houses were involved. And it is getting scarier."

"How?"

"You know where Claxton Elementary School is. It's twenty minutes from my school. Do you remember hearing about a drug bust near the school?"

"Vaguely."

"It wasn't an ordinary bust. Right in front of the school, police stopped a van that was driving erratically. They discovered a portable meth lab."

"A what?"

"A portable meth lab. All of the ingredients, the stove, everything was in the back of that van. Two guys and a woman were driving their explosive poison around in traffic. They didn't care about anyone's safety, including the kids in that school."

How do you respond to insanity? I used every indignant, sympathetic cliché I could think of. It was the beginning of my education. Jessica, always the teacher, shared facts and figures and horror stories with me. Over time, she would show me the "before" pictures of attractive people who became addicted. The "after" pictures showed gaunt, skeletal faces with eyes that seemed out of focus. They lost their teeth, and their skin filled with lesions, festering sores and scabs, exit wounds for escaping resins and toxins. They lost their homes, their families, and their jobs. They lost their dignity.

Donna Jo had lost the daily visits from her teacher. She had gained Miss Leena. It did not matter what the rest of her name was. Miss Leena was the nurse who had decided Donna Jo needed her considerable talents. She was a small, gray-headed, ebony-skinned dynamo with a gold-capped tooth and a gold-filled heart. She might not speak the King's English, but she was the queen of the I.C.U. where Donna Jo was resting. She would become the only person we could confide in when it came to our hopes and fears about her patient.

The first time we met her she told us, "Lawd God, I just about give up on hopin' for anyone to visit this child. I sure thought she was abandoned or somephin'. It is a pleasure to meet you."

There was something so basic and honest and good about her that, by the end of the first visit, we had shared information rarely shared with someone we had just met. When she learned of Jessica's role in Donna Jo's life, there was instant camaraderie. We began what would become a weekly pilgrim to Ohio, with almost daily phone calls either from or to Miss Leena. Jessica slept easier, knowing that Donna Jo had this compassionate woman watching over her. Miss Leena made life tolerable again.

CHAPTER 7

Shriners

Or: Wake Up Call

Sometimes I am amazed at how much I don't know. Not that I think I'm some brainiac. In fact, by now, I should be used to the concept. I call it immaculate misconception. Still, for a college graduate who works in a bookstore and loves to read, there are times when I don't know: a) squat b) jack c) jack-squat d) shit. I don't even know where those phrases come from, although Jack Squat could be some historical figure, like Jack Sprat.

I was reminded of my mental short comings (are there any long comings?) when we began visiting the Shriners Hospital. I don't know what they have against apostrophes, but I do know that I was clueless about their incredible work. I guess I just thought about those funny hats, and the stereotype comedians use when they talk about them at conventions, like these dorky guys who go all crazy when they get away from home and their wives.

Whenever people make those kinds of statements and I don't know any better I just seem to go along with them. I'm like a bobble head doll, just going yup, yup, yup, my head bobbling along, no thinking taking place at all. It's kind of pathetic.

I'd never thought about a Shriners Hospital. Never knew what wonderful institutions they are. Then I visited one. One of the twenty-two that exist. One of the best places for burn victims in the world. One of the hospitals that take in children like Donna Jo and treats them without charging anything. Free. Not one cent. They'd been doing so for decades, and I never knew enough to appreciate that incredible contribution to humanity. I knew more about Charles Manson than I did about the Shriners. What does that say?

Maybe you really don't know or appreciate something until it affects you. All I know is that Shriners Hospital in Cincinnati touched my heart.

Donna Jo should have been sent there immediately. She would have been sent there, but her doctors in Knoxville were afraid she wouldn't be able to make it. They were afraid she might die. But she eventually had to get there, and she did survive the trip, and in the process I became less clueless about a truly remarkable organization. They treat kids—severely burned kids—for free. Amazing. Maybe someone should build a shrine to the Shriners. Maybe I should be less of a bobble head.

CHAPTER 8

Blessings

Or: What If?

The ride to Cincinnati became a weekly ritual. We would leave Knoxville in the late afternoon and arrive four hours later, usually before ten. We would spend most of Saturday in the hospital, occasionally cruising the riverfront area in the evening. We'd make a quick visit on Sunday morning, then travel back to East Tennessee. Miss Leena usually worked on Saturday, but never on Sunday.

I got used to the drive. I got used to the hospital and its smells and sounds. I never got used to visiting an innocent young girl who should be blowing dandelions and painting pictures that showed a small house and a large dog and a yellow sun.

I especially got used to Miss Leena's down home love. Every time she gave us an update of Donna Jo's condition, she felt compelled to end it with, "Bless her little heart." It was the way she said heart that touched me. Like most Southerners, she drew the word out. It wasn't exactly two syllables, but it was more than one. It sounded like, "haaarrt," only there was a slight rising inflection at the end; not a full-fledged question, just a slight up turn of the voice.

It took a long time for me to grasp the two types of Southern heart blessings. In fact, if Jessica hadn't spelled it out, I might never have caught on. When many say, "Bless her heart," it's a euphemism, a way of criticizing or cussing without doing so. A prim and proper lady saying, "Bless her heart, she just doesn't have a clue" is really complaining about the good-for-nothing-so-and-so, maybe with occasional bleep thrown in, but she is doing it ever so politely. Adding, "Lord 'a Mercy" at the end might be an equally pleasant damnation.

Then there was the other type of blessing. When someone like Miss Leena looked at someone like Donna Jo and blessed her little heart, there never was or will be a purer or more sincere expression of compassion. I was sure Donna Jo would get better; anyone whose heart had been blessed as often as hers couldn't help but get better.

I hadn't tried a rematch of bobble head ping-pong, not since the last one ended so poorly. I wasn't sure how long the statute of my limitations required me to wait; I just knew that I hadn't reached it yet. Instead, on this particularly pleasant Sunday, Jessica chose to quiz me on all the things I had learned since leaving the North. Since she was driving, I took my time, looking at the passing countryside.

"I learned that the Tennessee landscape is full of hollers, and bottoms, and skeeters. I learned that Rocky Top is a sacred hymn, that people take very seriously the idea of truly being a part of the volunteer state, and that nothing should be planned on church night Wednesday or football Saturday."

By now, Jessica was smiling. I couldn't tell if she was being a teacher, reviewing her lessons, or just giving me a hard time. "What about being a bloody Yankee?"

"Ah yes, the Yankee. I learned that some of those people I thought were teasing or joking about my Yankeeness were actually telling truths in jest. Especially those who said, 'He can't help it, he's a Yankee, bless his heart.' I didn't realize that geographical prejudice ran rampant."

"Anything else?"

"I guess I learned that the South doesn't have a monopoly on prejudice or friendliness, that people care a lot about other people's religion, that sweet tea and barbeque and biscuits and gravy and fried chicken and red velvet cake and banana puddin' and blackberry cobbler are as good as it gets here in God's country. Oh yeah, I learned to say 'God's country' with the proper tone and reverence."

"Okay, that's enough, for now. I may want to review more at a later date. Right now, I'm thinking about something else."

"That's fine, but I have learned one other lesson I'd like to mention. I have learned that I can live anywhere as long as you are there, that geography is not important, and that your love means everything."

She took her right hand off the wheel, and for a short time we drove in silence, holding hands. I knew that my words had touched her. When the proper time had passed, she put her hand back on the steering wheel, gripping it hard before asking, "What happens if Donna Jo's mother dies?"

I wasn't surprised by the question, only the timing. I doubt if she was surprised by the response. "I will do whatever you want. That includes adoption if there are no other relatives." Before she could state the obvious, I added, "Yes, I know, if there were any relatives who cared we would have seen them already. But we both know the strange way our judicial system operates."

Her grip loosened on the steering wheel. After an hour we changed drivers, but not the conversation. We played the "what if" game all the way home

When she wants to, Jessica can lay on the Southern accent and the corresponding charm. After a long ride home, as Jessica got ready for bed, she used her Grand Ole Opry voice to say, "Bless Donna Jo's little heart, and Miss Leena's, too." Then, with that playful smile I hadn't seen lately, she whispered, "And bless my sweet husband's ever lovin' heart as well." With that, she was in my arms. It was better than any Julianne Moore/George Clooney dream. Maybe I'll write about that in my Great American Novel (hereafter, the G.A.N.)

CHAPTER 9

A Death Not in the Family
Or: Funeral Flashbacks

Donna Jo's mother died three days later. I have no idea of the specific, medical cause. Meth induced stupidity is not an official cause of death, although it should be. I also have no idea about the funeral. I must admit, my first reaction was sadness. I was pleasantly surprised. I feared I might feel relief, or worse, happiness. I didn't. My second reaction also surprised me, although not as pleasantly. I felt, I'm not exactly sure what to call it, some kind of queasy-producing, intangible emotion that wasn't exactly fear, wasn't exactly dread, and wasn't exactly anxiety. It wasn't exactly a premonition either, but I knew that this one death might launch a series of actions, and maybe equal and opposite reactions, that could lead to happiness or heartbreak. My protective instincts were on red alert, although for the life of me I don't know why I'd use a phrase like "red alert". I guess because it sounds better than, "fuchsia alert", or "vermillion".

"They say," whomever the ubiquitous and nefarious they are, that you never forget your first love. I guess that's true, but it is equally true that you never forget your first funeral. In my case, that first experience with death is far more vivid and meaningful than any first love.

Isaiah Jackson was the first black person I had ever met. It seems that even in liberal Massachusetts, we weren't always integrated. Isaiah was involved in our youth sports programs. We competed against each other in some sports, with each other in others. He was quiet, yet funny when he felt comfortable. I never thought about how uncomfortable it must have been for him, not until much later.

We were ten years old when Isaiah went on an overnight trip with the all-star traveling team. There is something wrong with creating all-stars at that age, but it happened; in fact, it still does. This isn't sour grapes either, I made the team, but I couldn't go because I was just getting over the measles. I was the most upset all-star in America, benched by a childhood disease. The day after the team left, we got the news. The team had stayed in a fancy hotel, complete with a swimming pool. It seems that the team was having a great time, running and diving and splashing. There was no lifeguard on duty, and for a while, no one noticed the young boy who, the autopsy would reveal, must have slipped or stumbled and hit his head on the side of the pool before falling in. By the time he was found, it was too late. Isaiah Jackson had become a drowning victim.

It took almost a week for the burial to occur. By then, I wasn't contagious. The entire team attended. My dad drove a car full of kids. There are three things I remember as clearly as I would if they had just happened. The first was seeing a dead body—a dead body that was my age. Isaiah didn't look totally real. His skin was lighter, and he looked almost plastic. Yet he also looked like he might wake up and play ball with us. The fact that he couldn't, ever again, took a long time to sink in.

It would take a long time, and several deaths, before I realized that the loud cries of grief and agony were not a part of more subdued white funerals. The wailing and falling and fainting of my first funeral constituted the second vivid memory, one that has never been duplicated in all of the death and tragedy I have faced.

The third memory was, in some ways, the worst. Chris Tanner was a big-mouthed, cocky shortstop most of us hated, even if he was our best hitter. We had watched the funeral, watched the dirt cover the casket, watched his family and friends overcome with grief. We were almost to the car when he interrupted the somber introspection we were all sharing, even if we were too young to know what somber introspection was. "You know what sucks?"

I thought it was one of those obvious questions, since we had just been to a funeral. Instead, Chris informed us, "Isaiah died owing me five bucks."

I wanted to pummel him, to really hurt him. I wanted to tell him I'd go ask his mother for the money. I wanted to give him five dollars and tell him not to worry about it, only I had no money. Instead, I called him an asshole. I hadn't been cussing all that long, but I believe I delivered the word quite well. It was the first time I ever swore in front of my father, who made sure to chastise me in front of everyone. I silently called him an asshole, also. I wouldn't have cared, except he said not one word to Chris, although his presence probably saved me from getting beat up. Chris was an idiot, but he was a strong idiot, at least at ten.

I often wondered what happened to Chris. What becomes of a ten-year-old who worries about money at a funeral? He probably grows up to be a politician. I think of these things almost every time someone I'm close to dies. I don't know why. Even the death of Donna Jo's mother, who I wasn't close to at all, made me remember it.

Jessica felt strange when she got the news, almost a sense of guilt for talking about adopting a child before the mother had died. Of course she was only being practical, but she felt guilty anyway, although not so guilty that she didn't begin what would become the nightmare of trying to adopt Donna Jo.

CHAPTER 10

Dadhood

Or: The Missionary Position Paper

I don't deal well with bureaucracy. Fortunately, Jessica, who also hates the bureaucratic b.s., somehow is able to handle it. She found a lawyer, a young woman name Theresa Covington, and the two of them got the ball rolling, jumped through the first hoop, and did other clichéd stuff to begin the process. Occasionally, I tagged along, but usually Jessica went alone. She didn't mind, as long as she knew I supported her.

I did support her. But I also found myself having tremendous bouts of insecurity, anxiety, and self-doubt. I was over forty. I liked my life. I didn't know the first thing about raising a child. I wanted to adopt Donna Jo because I knew it was the right thing to do. I knew that Jessica was Donna Jo's best hope for a normal life. I knew it would fill the hole that existed in my wife's life, that it would somehow make her feel whole, complete, maternal. But I was going to be a dad, and I wondered if I'd suck at it. I had always been critical of my parents, and Jessica's. I hated most of the little league parents I had met. I saw more than my share of spoiled brats and obnoxious parents at my store. Would I be any better? I was starting to think it was easy to be a critic when you didn't have a child of your own.

How would Donna Jo refer to me? Would she like me? Would I be able to talk to her? What about discipline? I began to worry about smaller, more specific concerns. What if she wet the bed? Or threw up? Or didn't like Atticus? I never once mentioned these thoughts to Jessica, which was strange. Other than occasional lurid dreams and fantasies, I never kept anything from her. Maybe I didn't want her to have to deal with one more problem. Maybe I didn't want her to see my insecurities, especially when I knew she would be such a wonderful mother. Maybe I was embarrassed about being such a wimp.

My more immediate problem was trying to slow down Jessica. I tried to tell her that Donna Jo might be in the hospital for many more months, that there was no guarantee about the adoption process, and that if it did go our way, it would still take many months to finalize. In her mind, Jessica knew I was right, but in her heart, it didn't matter. She wanted to convert our bland, spare bedroom into a homecoming haven for a little girl who had suffered big league trauma. She wanted to buy clothes and toys and books and games. Usually, I willed myself to share in her excitement, to help her in any way that I could. Yet somehow, somewhere in that inner sanctum of the cranial house of logic, I kept worrying that she might be setting herself up for a colossal disappointment. I had this nagging dread, the kind I use to get when I stayed home alone the first few times, the kind that says, "Someone is out there." Those fears proved to be false, and I hoped this one would, also. Still, I could not shake it.

Jessica knew five-year-olds. She didn't know ten-year-olds, and she didn't know that post-pubescent monster known as the teenager. I found myself waking up to the "what-ifs." What if Donna Jo had lasting damage from the fire? What if she turned to drugs, or got pregnant at fifteen, or resented us as wicked stepparents? What if her presence created a strain in our marriage? Where was the Julianne Moore dream when I needed it?

Of course, the biggest "what if" was the cruelest; what if this adoption did not happen? The ramifications of that reality would be unthinkable, so I tried not to think about it. I was not a worrier by nature. I had always hated my mother's perpetual state of angst. I saw it smother her, reduce her to an unpleasant bore who did nothing of substance, who went nowhere, who became a prisoner to her fears. I came to realize that it was worry that caused her to be so "set in her ways." That's why she hated change, the South, Jessica's accent, and anything that wasn't in keeping with her strict religious views. I swore I would never be that consumed or that conflicted. But the potential adoption of Donna Jo Crawford created my own special angst, and the potential non-adoption of Donna Jo Crawford left me concerned and conflicted and consumed.

Fortunately, there was work. We were constantly busy, lining up book signings and local acoustic guitar players and readings from local authors. The displays were always changing, as was the menu in our coffee shop. Former best-selling C.D.s had to make their way to the special values section, and then the discount rack. I found myself doing something else I swore I would never do. I was seeking escape, even refuge in my work. It was one of those things my father had done, one of the many things that made me dislike him. Now I was being just like him. I long ago realized that I loved my parents, if for no other reason than you almost have to love your parents. They did provide for me. I ended up with a college education and a good life. I honestly think they did the best they could. So I loved them, but I never liked them, or what they stood for. And that was my fear in this whole Donna Jo thing. I feared that, when she was an adult, she might view me the way I view them. I wasn't sure I could handle that kind of hurt.

Fortunately, there was "the humor," the humor that abounds in our home and our job and our world if we only know how and where to find it. Maybe my Great American Novel (hereafter, the G.A.N.) should be a comedy. Maybe it was time to stop parenthetically using G.A.N.

Derek and Amy Pearson are our closest friends. Our friendship is like some cosmic tide. At high tide, we are always together—sharing events and activities, enjoying each other's company. Then the tide recedes, and we go for long periods without seeing each other. We had been at such a low tide for some time. Fortunately, like the fluctuating ocean, it was only a matter of time before our friends returned.

I was able to convince Jessica that we needed to care about us. We needed a break from the weekly Cincinnati journey that was so stressful and exhausting. She called Miss Leena, who agreed to call us if there was any change, and called our friends to arrange a quiet Friday of beer and pizza at our place.

It began beautifully. Derek is a high school teacher who regales us with his stories from the classroom. If anyone should write a book, he should. He teaches kids who have been labeled "slow," or "low level," or "reluctant learners." He has preached passionate sermons about the damage those labels do to kids, but his words have fallen on deaf ears. He has had numerous offers to teach the "advanced" classes, but prefers to remain where he is. Maybe it's for the humor.

On this particular night, Derek began with a story too funny to be made up. It seems that his English class was reviewing for a *Julius Caesar* test by asking each other questions. He had turned it into a competition. One of his more intellectual students asked another about the nationality of the characters in the play. This required an explanation of the word nationality. Derek was hysterical as he imitated his thoughtful student. "Wait," the young man yelled, "I think I've got it. The play takes place in Rome, right?" When Derek assured him that, yes indeed, the play was set in Rome, the student, almost giddy with his sense of accomplishment, loudly proclaimed, "Then they were Romanians."

It is hard to argue with that kind of logic. Later that week, a student told him how excited he was about the upcoming "pepper rally." He even repeated one of our favorite stories, the one about the young lady who was trying to be creative in her original short story. She wanted to describe the ceiling fan as it spun, but instead of using the work oscillating, she went in to great detail about the ovulating fan. It was a classic. Of course, Derek had fun laughing at those gems, but if anyone else made fun of his students, he'd become as protective as hell, however protective that is.

Amy was ever bit as funny as her husband. She was a nurse who specialized in neonatal care. Initially, it was awkward when she talked about all the newborns she saw. She sensed this, and she and Jessica had numerous discussions about Jessica's childless condition. Derek and Amy also had two children of their own, both of them in college. Somehow, they were able to talk about their children without being obnoxious about it; obnoxious being from the point of view of adults without children. Amy's best moment of the week was funny in a pitiful sort of way. She was standing at the nurse's station when an expectant mother and her husband arrived, the latter carrying a suitcase. When Amy asked if she could help them, the mother-to-be informed her that she had come to have her baby. Amy asked if she were in labor, and the woman seemed confused, only saying that it was time for her baby. Amy asked about contractions, the woman repeated her mantra about the baby. The non-communication tango might have continued its absurdity if Amy weren't so perceptive. She asked, "Is today your due date?" When the woman smiled and nodded, thinking she had finally gotten through to this dense nurse, Amy continued, "So you thought ..." she couldn't or wouldn't finish the thought.

It was almost comical, in fact, we were all laughing at this point; laughing at the expense of the deep thinker who showed up on her due date ready to have the baby. Only it really wasn't funny, especially when Amy described how hurt and disappointed the lady was after Nurse Pearson explained the other facts of life and birth. She and her husband left, holding hands, shaking their heads as they retreated from the nursing station. Amy's assurance that they would, indeed, have a baby soon did little to comfort them.

It is especially important for kindergarten teachers to have adult conversations. Jessica was acutely aware of that fact. While she had close teacher friends, it was Amy she confided in, Amy's opinion that mattered, Amy who she trusted. As the beer flowed and the pizza ebbed, if ebbed means "was devoured," the conversation turned to Donna Jo. Amy was the proverbial wealth of knowledge, about meth, about burns, about the dangers that still lie ahead in the recovery process. She was factual, providing warnings and comfort and encouragement in equal doses. The conversation often meandered like a brook, lazily rolling on to shallow topics like sports or current events or my work, but eventually returning to the deeper topic of adoption. It was a nice evening, and should have stayed that way. It would have stayed that way if I were a better host.

Derek is a good man, a man I respect in so many ways. He is also a religious man. On some level, I respect that, also. He's not a fanatic, hell, he was drinking beer and laughing with me. But when he ended our latest Donna Jo discussion with what I perceived as a dismissive and simplistic, "God has a plan for you and Donna Jo. You'll see," I lost it. "It" in this case refers to social graces. Maybe I should say I lost them.

"So God's responsible for Donna Jo lying in intensive care in the burn unit of Shriners Hospital? Is God now in charge of the legal system? What, did He take over after the O.J. verdict?"

"Adam, that's not …"

Jessica tried to calm me down, but I didn't want to hear it. "No. I'm sick of this. You're busting your ass filling out papers and meeting with lawyers. We drive to Cincinnati and back almost every weekend. We agonize over a girl whose parents almost killed her (unless God did it), and we watch her black blisters ooze and fester. We are trying to do the right thing, and I'll be damned if I think God is controlling this." I could have continued, but when I paused for a breath I noticed the looks on the three faces that were staring at me. I decided to quit, allowing the awkward silence to wash over all of us.

Amy spoke first. "So, how do you think the Vols will do next year?" It was a valiant attempt. I ignored the angry eye contact Jessica was trying to make. Amy continued, "I'll bet they'll be fine if they settle on a quarterback."

Thanks to Amy, the silence was slightly less awkward than meeting Jessica's parents for the first time. I heard my wife speak, and Derek, but all I heard were words. I gathered no information. I think I mumbled something as I stood up. I found myself walking, walking across the floor and out the door and into the backyard, as if some external force was in control of my body and my movements. I didn't truly recognize or realize where I was and what I was doing until I opened the kennel door and Atticus came bounding out. I held

Atticus as I heard our guests leave, then I released him so he could greet Jessica as she walked toward us. For a long time she allowed the scene to play out. I leaned against the kennel, alternating between anger and some unknown emotion. I was angry with Derek. I was angry with myself. I was angry with myself for being angry with Derek, and I was angry with myself for being angry with myself. I was angry at anger itself, but there was something else, something undefinable. I began to cry. To this day I don't know why. I looked at my house and my wife and my dog, and perhaps I feared that I might lose them, or perhaps I feared I had lost my best friend, or perhaps I feared that Derek might be right. I don't know when Jessica noticed my tears. In one of those situations where you are a main participant but don't really understand or appreciate the fact, I vaguely remember Atticus being returned to his kennel and Jessica taking my hand and the two of us somehow arriving in the kitchen. Then, suddenly, there was clarity.

This was the second time Derek and I had had a not so religious war. The first had been at his house after, coincidentally, beer and pizza. Maybe it wasn't a coincidence. Maybe pizza makes a person say things he might regret later.

Derek had gone on at considerable length about the missionary trips so many of his students had experienced. I finally interrupted him. "You mean conversion trips?" Initially, he didn't understand the question, so I elaborated. "Missionary trip, as a phrase sounds so noble and benign. Let's call it what it is—a conversion trip, a trip to convert 'heathens' to a specific way of thinking."

We debated the issue in a semi-friendly manner, and it could have ended just fine until I did what I seem to do best, or worst. I went too far. I said that I hoped that somewhere in some Muslim country, someone was organizing a "missionary" trip to Tennessee, where so many infidels were in need of conversion. I told him I fully expected all good Baptists to greet them with open minds and arms.

That was the first test of our friendship. We survived this mild jihad and agreed to disagree. I said all the things a person says after such an event, and even though I still think it was an interesting point, I really didn't mean to be offensive. I gained tremendous respect for the way Derek seemed to truly forgive and forget.

From that time until now, we had never had a serious disagreement. Now, it had happened again, and I felt terrible. I didn't feel so terrible about what I had said, but I hated my approach, my combative, sanctimonious attitude. I, who claim to be open-minded, was antagonistic about another man's belief. And Derek was not a phony, nor was he trying to force his beliefs on anyone else. I went to my computer, and wrote an email that said all of that and more. It was a sincere effort at explanation and apology. I sent it to Derek, knowing that he tended to stay up late, knowing that he spent those late hours on the computer, and hoping that he would read it before going to bed.

Jessica read the email, and that was all she needed. She went to bed, alone. I had a few more hours of self-flagellation to finish. Why had I snapped at my friend? It would be so easy if it was because of the beer, or because I didn't like the people, or because I felt attacked. None of that was the case. It was my prejudice talking. That would take some getting used to, or some changing.

CHAPTER 11

The Day After

Or: Anatomy 101

It was 8:00 when I awoke. For me, that's sleeping in, although I actually slept out—in my cushiony chair by the fireplace. The way Atticus greeted my "lateness" let me know that he would chastise me if dogs were capable of doing so. By the time I took care of him and showered, I was starving. That's when the doorbell rang.

I opened the door and received one of the greatest gifts I have ever been given. It was the gift of forgiveness. Amy and Derek were standing there, loaded down with coffee and bagels and pastry and Amy's homemade sausage balls. Derek started to apologize for bringing coffee from one of my store's competitors, but I waved him off. I started to apologize for ruining what had been an enjoyable evening, but he waved me off. "Your email said it all. Case closed."

I thanked him, hugged him, and told him I treasured his friendship. That's when Amy waved us both off by hugging me while saying, "If you two don't mind, I'm hungry." By the time we had everything arranged on the table, Jessica had joined us. It was the perfect morning after, a simple yet profound gesture that could not have touched me more. I told Derek that as he left. He smiled and told me that he was still going to pray for me. I smiled and told him I could use all the help I could get.

I hated feeling like a horse's ass. I also hated the fact that it was a horse's anatomy that became synonymous with being an idiot. Why the horse? Horses are noble, regal beasts. Why wasn't I acting like an elephant's ass? It would be bigger. Or an iguana's ass? It would be more "low down." Even a cow's ass would make more sense than a horse's ass. I decided that, from now on, whenever I was being stupid, I was going to call myself a cow's ass. Besides, I like the symmetry between cow's ass and bullshit.

The first day after I've been a cow's ass is almost like learning to walk again. I'm a little shaky. Every event seems to remind me of my latest cow's assiness. I'm wobbly, in need of time, time that separates me from the event, time that allows me to get my confidence back, to feel like an adult again.

I knew there was a great deal of bigotry fostered by religion. Now I had to ask the question, "Am I a bigot against religion, or those who are religious?" I decided that if I was, I needed to stop it, because bigotry is bigotry. I made an Old Year's Resolution, because the year was almost over, to be the kind of open-minded man I used to think I was. I also resolved to give myself a break. If Derek could forgive me, then I could certainly forgive myself. It was another step toward distancing myself from the event. In a few days I would forget about what a cow's ass I had been, at least until the next time.

CHAPTER 12

The Call

Or: It Doesn't Take Much

Jessica had been done with school for two weeks when the call came. We had just finished supper, or dinner, depending on your upbringing, when the phone rang. I was three feet away when my wife motioned for me to listen in. We have a speakerphone. Not once have we used the speaker. We stood together, listening to Miss Leena say, "There is someone who wants to talk to you."

It could only be one person. We listened as Miss Leena held the phone for her patient and urged her to speak. Then we heard the soft, halting, almost robotic voice. "Hell … o … Miss … es … Don … a … hue." It sounded forced, almost metallic, and yet, it was the most beautiful sound either of us had ever heard.

"Hello Donna Jo. It is good to hear your voice."

"Thank … you … ma'am."

"My husband and I have been to see you almost every weekend. Did you know that?"

"Yes … ma'am. Miss … Lee … na … told … me."

"And I'll bet Miss Leena is taking good care of you isn't she?"

"Yes … um."

"Do you know what day it is?"

"No … um."

"It's Thursday. Adam, that's my husband, and I will see you on Saturday. That's the day after tomorrow. Will that be okay?"

"I ... I'd ... like ... that ... very ... much."

"Why don't you get some rest and let me talk to Miss Leena. I'll see you soon, honey."

"Good ... bye ... ma'am."

"Good-bye, sweetie."

I don't know how my wife did it. She was trembling and teary-eyed during the entire conversation, but her voice remained perfectly clear and controlled. When Miss Leena took the phone, Jessica's voice quivered. "Thank you so much. She's doing so much better, isn't she?"

Neither of us expected the pause, nor the answer. "Are you going to be home for a while?"

"Yes."

"Let me call you back after awhile."

Awhile turned out to be almost an hour, during which time we relived the joys of the surprise call, and speculated about Miss Leena would tell us.

When the phone call came, Miss Leena explained that she had not wanted to talk in front of Donna Jo. She said the doctors were encouraged by her being awake and talking, and they thought her skin was doing fine. Then, Miss Leena told us something Amy had warned us about. The doctors were "very concerned." Those were Miss Leena's exact words. They were very concerned about internal damage. The extent to which the smoke and the chemicals had harmed Donna Jo's organs, especially her lungs, was still undetermined. There were many days of testing awaiting her.

Miss Leena had not been trying to alarm us. She just wanted to keep us informed. I wondered if she had waited for something so positive to happen before telling us, maybe to maintain some balance, but I never asked. Even though the phone call warned of potential danger, we were not pessimistic when we hung up. Nothing, not even future problems, could dampen our excitement. Donna Jo had spoken, and we had every reason to believe she would speak again, in person, on Saturday.

CHAPTER 13

Like Riding a Bike

Or: More Anatomy

I never once used training wheels. Not one time. In fact, I taught myself how to ride a bike. There was no Hallmark™ moment, no dad running along side, nervously letting go as I soloed for the first time. I learned how to balance by riding next to the curb. I fell, scraped my knee and my elbow, but I kept going. I was proud of that.

I got the bike for Christmas. Christmas in Massachusetts. I couldn't take it outside until March. By May, I was riding. Dear old dad kept promising to put the training wheels on and to teach me, but of course he never go around to it. In a way, I'm glad. I suppose it would have been nice to have a father spending "quality time" with me, teaching me to ride a bike and throw a ball and catch a fish. But I'm kind of happy that I learned these things for myself.

I do wish someone had taught me about sex. I believed every myth every classmate perpetuated. It never occurred to me that they might be as ignorant as I was. I remember the first breasts I ever saw. They were glossy, shiny, and magnificent. I believe it was Miss October. A boy never forgets a moment like that. Fingers Costanzo had borrowed one of his old man's *Playboys*. Fingers did not get his great nickname from a gangster movie, nor did it have anything to do with stealing. As far as I know, the only things Fingers ever filched were magazines, and he was not very good at that. His father caught him when he tried to purloin Miss November. Fingers became Fingers because of a special talent—his ability to break wind seemingly at will. It was his unique version of the ancient, "pull my finger" routine. We never tired of it, at least not for the first 83,000 times. We'd go looking for unsuspecting people. We loved it when a new kid moved in. We even got him to try it out on our librarian, ol' Mrs. Kane. She didn't see the humor, and Fingers got in trouble for that one.

When we got to high school, and started trying to date the girls we used to pick on (or gross out completely), Fingers seemed to lose his magic. I was there the day his finger was pulled and silence followed. It was a sad day in our lives. Fingers was over-the-hill, washed-up, a has-been. Someone said that he was just pooped-out, and we thought that was so funny we repeated it for days, laughing like we were hearing it for the first time. I realize now that Fingers was just tired of the same old routine. Maybe he grew up before the rest of us. Of course, if you're going to date, the pull my finger routine isn't exactly the best pick up line.

Fingers never lost the nickname, not in high school. For a while, whenever new people would ask him why he was called Fingers, he would say that he was learning to play the piano. Then he started dating seriously, and the rumor was that he found a new reason for the nickname, although I have no way of knowing that. Fingers and I drifted apart. Once he became a ladies man, there was no way he could hang out with those of us who didn't stand a chance with the opposite sex. The reason we didn't stand a chance was because we were scared to death. Calling, writing notes, actually speaking to a female in person was more thrilling than hang gliding, more dangerous than climbing Mount Everest in the winter.

Eventually, all of us losers actually did get dates. They just weren't the kind of swinging sexual forays we had heard about. Ours was the long, scenic route to sexual fulfillment, with long stopovers at the hand holding and kissing stages, a few detours to the copping a feel through the heavy sweater phase, and an occasional break through to touching actual skin.

I think it was during one of those reminiscences, no doubt with Atticus by my side, when my fear of paternity began to evaporate. If Donna Jo could overcome the severe and painful damage done to her body, and perhaps her mind, if Jessica and Theresa could fight the legal battles that might lead to adoption, I could certainly overcome my self-doubt. I would teach Donna Jo to ride a bike, or throw a ball, or any other thing she wanted. I would talk to her about sex, just because I know what being in the dark feels like. And if Donna Jo ever wanted to go to the beach, we'd go, and we'd swim together, and I'd make sure she knew all about jellyfish.

CHAPTER 14

The Blues

Or: Separate Ways

Our trip to Cincinnati began with such high hopes. Jessica had spoken with Donna Jo just days earlier. There was the certainty that she would be even better, that we would talk in person, that her progress would be obvious. Both of us are, at least occasionally, perceptive enough to know that progress is rarely linear. As much as we would like it to be so, improvements rarely happen in a straight line. Often, there are starts and stops, improvements and setbacks. That is true of historical change, societal advancement, and the recuperation of a little girl in a hospital. Knowing that did little to cushion our disappointment. Donna Jo would not be speaking today.

"Coma" is a four-letter word, one of the dirtiest four letter words I know. We had avoided saying it ever since the ordeal began, but Miss Leena told us, "Yesterday, she was talkin' right fine, but last night, the child just stopped, right sudden like. It's like she got tired, then slipped into a deep sleep. That's how comas are, ya just never know 'bout 'em."

The word just hung there, so intrusive and final. Coma. There was never a doubt in my mind what would happen next. We spent the day, talking to Donna Jo and, when she had a moment, Miss Leena. We went to the riverfront for some ribs and some music. It was late in the evening when Jessica broached the topic I had been anticipating. "I'm on my summer break. I'm thinking about something that you may not like."

I knew that, and she was right, selfishly, I didn't really like it, but I responded in the only way that made sense. "I love you."

"I know. I love you, too, and I don't want to be away from you, but I think I need to be here for awhile, not just on weekends."

We had rarely been apart. I can recall each lonely evening when a conference or a workshop required one of us to be away from home. Both of us hated it. It was one of the things that made our marriage so strong. Now, Jessica was talking about being away for who knows how long. I hated the idea. The only thing I hated more was the agony I knew Jessica was feeling for this child she loved. It was as pure and maternal and genuine as any love I had ever seen. How selfish would a husband have to be to deny that love?

"Adam, are you still there?"

"I'm here."

"You know I don't love you any less, don't you?"

"I do."

"So, you're okay with this?"

"I'm as okay as a man losing his love life can be. I'm just thinking what I'll do when Julianne Moore appears in my dreams and you're not there when I wake up."

"Maybe we should go back to the hotel and see if she'll appear tonight."

"I like the way you think."

"Adam, thank you. Thank you for understanding and supporting and, well, for loving me."

It was a beautiful evening, and a beautiful morning. We said good-bye to Donna Jo and Miss Leena later that afternoon. We drove back to Knoxville, spent another wonderful evening together, and woke up Monday morning to a harsh reality. I was going to work. Jessica was going to pack and drive to Cincinnati. My wife was leaving me, and even though it wasn't in the manner that most wives leave their husbands, it was a parting. Some people say that you never truly appreciate something until it's gone. Some people must be slow learners. Never once did I need absence to make my heart grow fonder. Never once did I need separation to appreciate Jessica. Walking into my house after work and not having her there was a new low in loneliness, especially when I knew that this time would be longer than any other time. Even Atticus seemed to miss her, although he received more attention than usual. It was the beginning of a long test, a test I was not always sure I could pass.

CHAPTER 15

Fillers

Or: Split Milk

I once got thrown off my school bus for hitting the bus driver in the head with a milk carton. In my defense, the milk carton was empty, and I was not trying to hit the bus driver. I guess that's really not much of a defense.

I was in sixth grade. Sixth grade is the top of the line in elementary school. It never occurred to us that next year, as seventh graders, we would be the low-life, bottom of the food chain group on the junior/senior high school bus. We were too busy being stupid. At least I was.

An annoying fifth grader (an A.F.G.) was sitting in the front seat. I was in the ultra-cool back seat. There was an empty milk carton on the floor. Some external force whispered, "Chuck it at the annoying fifth grader." I obeyed.

It probably would be a better story if I could remember the A.F.G.'s name, but I can't. All I know is that I wound up, let the carton fly, and watched it sail toward my target. Two things happened in perfect unison, they could not have been choreographed any better.

First, with the milk carton missile bearing down on his head, the oblivious A.F.G. bent down to get something he had placed on the floor. It was at that very second when Bad News Barney, our semi-sober bus driver, decided to bound up the stairs of the bus. He wasn't even on the top step when the aircraft met his forehead. It played out in slow motion, A.F.G. ducking, Barney coming into view, and the direct hit. I saw it all as I stood, frozen, in my perfect follow-through. It didn't take Sherlock Holmes to figure out who threw it. I spent some quality time with the principal, and my parents, and for two weeks I could not ride the bus. My dad drove me to school every morning; more quality time spent with an angry parent. I walked home every afternoon, almost two miles. It never snowed, there were no hills, and I actually enjoyed it. The walk home that is. The ride each morning was hell. I was amazed that a parent could be so consistently bitchy each and every morning.

I found myself telling Amy and Derek that story on the first evening of what would become a weekly ritual—Thursday dinner with the Pearsons. It became something I looked forward to—dinner with friends followed by a weekend with my wife. From the time I left Cincinnati on Sunday until Thursday evenings with Amy and Derek, little else mattered. Everything revolved around the next weekend, the next precious time I would spend with Jessica. And Donna Jo.

I had never spoken with Donna Jo. I visited, but she was never awake. I listened to the one phone call she had made, though I said nothing. Yet I found myself missing her, and caring about her. I watched her burned and scarred body, trying to imagine her pain and her fear. I saw her as courageous, just like my wife. I felt helpless, yet strangely inspired when I was in her presence. I discovered that it is possible to love someone before you ever talk to her.

So my Thursdays with Amy and Derek became "true confessions." As opposed to "false confessions". Sometimes I talked about milk cartons and bus drivers. Sometimes I talked about the intriguing little girl who had captured my heart. It was then that I was reminded of the almost spiritual bond of friendship. Amy and Derek fed me, took care of Atticus for me, and most importantly, they listened to me. I do not believe I would have made it through my separation from Jessica if not for them. I had friends, memories to share, and things to look forward to. Everything else was just "filler," "stuff" that had to be done so I could get to the good stuff. Stuff is a very technical term. Even my job seemed like filler.

CHAPTER 16

Vacation

Or: Candles

We had planned for years. We had saved for years. This was to be the year of the cruise—the Caribbean Cruise. We had booked the last two weeks of July. Fortunately, we had purchased cancellation insurance.

Instead of "the islands," I spent two glorious weeks in Cincinnati. Atticus went to a kennel, and I felt guilty every time I thought about that.

For two weeks I saw Jessica every day. For two weeks I studied Donna Jo's comatose face for the slightest sign of improvement. For two weeks we made Cincinnati as much of a vacation spot as we could. It was at the end of that time period that another life-altering decision was reached.

"I don't want to go back to school this fall. My heart isn't in it. It's here, with Donna Jo. I have enough sick leave built up that I can actually get the equivalent of a paid absence for the entire year. I've given this a lot of thought, Adam, and the only down side is the continued separation. I hate that, and I know you do, too. But Adam?"

"Yes?"

"I, I need you to understand something."

"Go on."

"You've heard all the political crap about raising standards?"

"You think it's crap?"

"I think it's a great theory, but it's not happening, especially the way it's being funded."

"What's that got to do with what we're talking about?"

"In my mind, everything. Take Donna Jo. Her parents were doing and selling meth. If she had stayed in that environment, had continued to breathe the air in her house, what chance did she really have?"

I shook my head, still uncertain where this was headed.

"School has become a testing factory. All we care about is the score on a standardized test. Even kindergarten teachers feel it. I don't like the atmosphere. But here's the thing. If I go back to school, Donna Jo will be left behind, in every way possible. There's just no bloody way I can leave her behind."

"Jessica, I, I mean, what if …" It was one of my more articulate responses. I wasn't sure if it was her use of the word bloody or my concern over another issue. It didn't matter, since my wife almost always knows what I'm thinking.

"I know. Maybe we lose the adoption battle, or the custody battle, as Theresa calls it. I'll be crushed. All I can do is what my heart tells me to do. But Adam, what if we win? What if Donna Jo becomes my daughter, our daughter? What is best for her?"

"You are best for her. Just like you are best for me."

"Adam, you know that my loving her doesn't diminish my love for you, don't you?"

Once again I was struck by my wife's uncanny ability to say exactly the right thing at the right time. Was I subconsciously feeling left out, perhaps even jealous of the attention Donna Jo was getting at my expense? I just might be, but as soon as that possibility was verbalized, I saw it for the enemy that it was, and banished it immediately. "I know that. I'm really not feeling left out." It was true, now.

My wife then repeated a quote she loved, although she couldn't remember its author. "A candle loses none of its own light by lighting other candles." She smiled at me, placing my hands in hers before adding, "I am that candle. The love I'm giving Donna Jo won't take from the love I have for you. And someday, when we are a family, there will be more light, more love. I hate not being with you every day, but it is temporary. What we are trying to do here may be the most important, lasting thing that we ever do."

And suddenly, there was clarity. I had just spent two weeks with my wife. I saw her every weekend. It was not ideal, but it was not the world's greatest tragedy, either.

When we got married, I was like all grooms, at least I suspected I was. I was "in love," with all the romantic repercussions of that phrase. I thought that no one had ever known love like mine, not before or since. It never dawned on me that love could grow, at least not initially. Love was love. If you were in it, that was it. Case closed. Only the case kept opening again.

I don't remember when I said it or even realized it for the first time. I just remember there coming a time when I knew as definitely as anything I had ever known, that I loved my wife more at that point in time than I did on my wedding day. It surprised me, and it continued to surprise me each time it reoccurred. Every parental death, every time we made up after a fight, every time she showed me love and understanding and kindness that was more than I deserved, although exactly what I hoped for. As I looked into Jessica's eyes, I once again became aware of that magical phenomenon. I truly loved her more at that moment than I had ever loved before. I told her that, and later that evening, I showed her that.

And suddenly, vacation was over. I was going back to Knoxville, and back to work. Jessica would continue her vigil, and her long distance legal preparation with Theresa. She would not be in the classroom in the fall, and that bothered me. She would try to do what no political edict could ever accomplish. She would make sure that Donna Jo Crawford, or maybe Donna Jo Donahue, would not be left behind. As for me, I couldn't wait to see Atticus.

CHAPTER 17

Doornails

Or: Witless Wisdom

"Are doornails deader than other nails?" Derek was on a roll, or a biscuit, or a bagel. It was Thursday. We had just finished a Thanksgiving-style dinner even though it was the last week in July. Derek and I were feeling the post pig-out discomfort; one we felt would be helped if we continued drinking the wine that had accompanied our feast. I knew Derek wasn't looking for a response, other than a laugh, which is what I gave him. He was animated; I was mellow. He was ready to talk; I was ready to listen. Amy was ready for bed, and went there.

"I heard a funny comment the other day." I wanted to interrupt him and ask what "the other day" actually meant, but I didn't. If it was anything like "the other woman," I didn't want to stop his rhythm. "One of our laziest teachers, the one who complains the most and does the least, was talking about how burned out he was becoming. I was getting tired of hearing it, but I wasn't about to say anything. I guess ol' Dotty Jamison was tired of hearin' it also, 'cause she looked at ol' Harry, that's the complainer's name, looked him right in the eye and said, 'Harry, in order to be burnt out, you first have to have been on fire. You are never gonna burn out.' I thought I was gonna die."

"What did Harry do?"

"Well, ol' Dotty said it like she was just tryin' to be funny, so Harry just laughed a little too loudly, and a moment later he remembered some work he had to do and left. We all laughed after he left."

It was a great story, one that was well told, complete with "ol'" for people who weren't old, and the one syllable "fire," and the sweet syrupy sound of a perfect Southern drawl. Derek wasn't done. He concluded, "I told Dotty I thought Harry was losing it, and she didn't miss a beat, just rolled her eyes and said, 'Honey, ol' Harry never had it.' Golly bum that woman is funny."

It was the grand finale, although I've never heard of any other kind of finale, like a mediocre finale or a pitiful finale. In fact, I've never heard of a grand beginning or a grand middle, only a finale. But any finale that contained golly bum in it had to be grand.

There was a momentary lull in the conversation, although I suspect that most lulls are momentary, otherwise they wouldn't be lulls. The lull ended with, "Adam, you've been quiet tonight. Is everything okay?"

"Yeah, it is, I'm just enjoying your stories and my turkey and wine—induced mellowness."

"Don't you have any cosmic insights into the world, any Dotty-like wit or wisdom?"

"You want wit or wisdom? Now?"

"Absolutely."

"Like what?"

"I don't know, like why is a number two pencil so special? What's wrong with number one?"

"Ah, you want deep thoughts."

"Yes."

"All of my thoughts seem shallow tonight, but here's one. What was the first straw?"

"What?"

"You know, everyone always says, 'That was the last straw.' I always want to know what the first straw was."

"Good one. I'll bet that took most of your forty odd years to learn."

Derek was a year younger than I, and he was not above reminding me of that. "Derek, age references aside, have you ever said, 'Your forty even years?' I mean, at 42, 44, 46, you still say forty-odd years. Isn't that a little weird?"

"Bravo! Brilliant! What else have you learned in your first half century?"

"I've learned not to pick up jellyfish."

"And?"

"And, that metal wrenches and car batteries can be hazardous to your knuckles. What about you, you've got almost half century of learnin', too?"

"I've learned that pet rocks and volcanic ash are best-selling items."

It was almost like a competition, and I was warming to the task. "I've learned that whenever someone tells me something for my own good it is never any good."

"At my school, they can require me, require me mind you, to do what they call optional in-service."

"I've learned, from our political leaders, that the bigger the screw-up, the bigger and bolder the subsequent lie must be."

"How about this? Airplane food and school cafeteria food are prepared by the same people, and both may be an oxymoron."

I smiled, tiring of the game. "My friend, I've learned that absence makes the weeks seem longer, that Thursday nights with you and Amy are sanity savers, and that weekend reunions are better than Julianne Moore dreams." That ended the game, if that is what it had been. We sat, basking in the friendship, neither wanting to disturb that fragile moment. Since it was only a moment, and since we both had that job thing to deal with, I disturbed it, rising to end another wonderful evening. I expressed my gratitude and went home, one step closer to seeing Jessica again.

CHAPTER 18

Woodwork
Or: Family Feud

July gave way to August, and August gave way to legal insanity, or more accurately, the insanity that is the legal system. Every time I turned around there was another form to complete. I tried not turning around, but the forms kept coming, along with representatives from every social service organization known to man (and a few unknown to man or woman). Jessica and I were investigated, examined, inspected, dissected, analyzed, probed, questioned, and interviewed. And interviewed. And interviewed. There were days when I felt like Arlo Guthrie facing his draft board.

Theresa assured us that it was all part of the process, and that everything was proceeding normally. In fact, she said things were moving quickly. I asked her if she thought evolution was an overnight phenomenon. She told me it was all part of our unique birthing process, our labor. I asked if we were going to have the gestation of an elephant. She indicated that a typical Homo sapien's timeframe was more likely.

Unfortunately, even Theresa could not predict the craziness that followed. Actually, as a lawyer, she probably could have predicted it, but chose not to share that prediction with us.

Suddenly, there was a custody fight, in fact, two of them. Theresa told us they were coming out of the woodwork. I loved that phrase. Not once have I ever heard of people going into the woodwork. Not once has anyone claimed to actually see someone going into the woodwork, yet everyone, including our lawyer, sees these people coming out of the woodwork. How did they get there?

I would loved to have spent more time contemplating the woodwork issue, but clearly the implications of here statement were more significant than my word games.

The first woodwork dwellers were Ernie Lee Lowe and his wife Janie. They were neighbors when the Crawford house was still standing. They just decided it was their duty to help that poor, sweet little child that, "Got blowed up." Theresa told Jessica not to worry, that they weren't a serious threat. I knew that didn't make my wife any less worried. I also wondered if there were non-serious threats. The second denizens of the woodwork were a serious threat, even in Theresa's eyes. Frank and Arlene Crawford were from Briceville, and they were family. "Kin" as the Crawfords like to say. And even though these kin had never once visited their relative, suddenly they wanted custody of her.

Theresa had done her best to prepare us for this possibility. She said it would be highly unusual if someone didn't step forward to contest our plan. We still weren't prepared, not now, not after all of this time. Jessica's initial reaction was hurt, as though she had been slapped, which in a figurative sense she had been. Her hurt gave way to anger, then to a surprisingly calm determination. "Tell me what happens next."

Theresa explained that there would be paperwork (what a surprise). There would be investigations of the two newly interested parties, just as we had been investigated. Eventually, there would be hearings, motions, counter-motions, sworn statements, and direct testimony and all kinds of legal ploys and posturing. It was not something to look forward to, especially when the potential for nastiness existed. All for a little girl who might never speak again, who had no say in this entire mess. Theresa said that is why she loved her job. She truly believed she was giving a voice to those who would otherwise remain unheard. I hoped she was right.

Just before the conversation ended, Jessica asked, "Why? Why the interest? Why now?"

I suspect Theresa had been waiting for that. "I hate to attribute motives to others, especially when there are so many possibilities. It could be that they are genuinely concerned, that they think they are doing the right thing."

Both of us started to protest, but she stopped us with her hand. "I know. I'm *your* lawyer. Remember? Anyway, it is a possibility. So is greed. Many times people are fishing—fishing for money."

"Money, from Donna Jo?"

"Money from insurance policies, bank accounts, property, anything they might be awarded in addition to the custody."

"But kids cost money, especially if they have medical bills, which Donna Jo may have after she leaves the hospital. Don't they know that?"

"Maybe. Maybe they don't care about that. Maybe they think there is a great sum of money. Trust me, the reasons are as varied as the people, and don't spend too much time looking for logic."

"Are we going to lose Donna Jo?"

"It's too early to tell."

"But you have a feel, an idea. What's your guess?"

Theresa took her time before carefully crafting her answer. "The neighbors, I'm not concerned with them. They have no more claim than you do, less if you consider all that you've done. The relatives, they're another story."

It has been my experience that every time something is "another story," that story is a bad one. Theresa's other story wasn't any different. "Courts, for obvious reasons, give preference to blood relatives. That's not to say it always goes that way, in fact there is some legal precedent in your favor, but most of the time, family trumps non-family."

"Even if the so-called family hasn't shown the least bit of interest in their own flesh and blood?"

"It's not a perfect system. Look, I'm on your side. Let me do my job. You do have one strong thing in your favor."

"What's that?"

"You've got me."

Somehow, she was able to say that without sounding the least bit conceited. Jessica smiled as they parted, but moments later there wasn't the slightest hint of a smile. I watched as she prepared herself for a battle she did not choose. I watched her compose herself, assuming a determined and confident outward appearance. I watched her mask a heart that I knew was breaking.

CHAPTER 19

The Calm

Or: Helping Children

"I'm coming home. I need to get out of here. I need to sleep in my own bed, with my husband. Let's go out for dinner."

It was a Tuesday morning, and my day could not have started better. Jessica was coming home. The fact that she sounded frustrated, or at least in need of some love and understanding from her husband made the anticipation even greater. Work dragged. Coming home to her was one of those simple pleasures that made life wonderful.

We dined out, then hurried home to share what had been missing, at least during the week, from our relationship. Sex … midweek … sleeping together … waking together. We even made love the next morning. I arrived at work only a few minutes before everyone else. It was the latest I've ever been early. I even got caught in the Kingston Pike crawl, but I was still smiling, even in the traffic. I remember thinking that life is all about four-letter words, and not just the ones I saw being mouthed by the Kingston Pike crawlers. There were the dirtiest of four letter words, like coma and hate and fear and hurt. But there were the beautiful ones, also. Words like home and safe and love and wife. Especially wife. Wife may be the best word I have ever heard.

Beer is also a four-letter word, and on Friday night, as an attempt to show our appreciation for all of the Thursday night meals, Derek and Amy were cordially invited to a beer and lobster and shrimp and steak bash at our house. Bash is also a four-letter word, but it isn't quite to the wife level. I promised I would not be a cow's ass this time, a promise I kept. Jessica spent the day preparing. She said it had been so long since she cooked anything it was actually enjoyable. Her efforts produced a meal we would talk about for years to come. In fact, it became the measuring stick for future bashes.

If, as Ben Franklin so eloquently stated, "Beer is God's way of showing that he loves us and wants us to be happy," than lobster is Mother Nature's way of doing the same. We felt loved and happy and bloated when the last claw had been cracked, the last butter dipped succulent tail devoured. Derek had just finished telling us about a student who got in a fight because another student called him a thespian. The kid yelled, "I'm not gay," and started punching the other student. That's when the phone rang.

I watched Jessica answer the phone with her Southern charm and grace, a smile accompanying her words. I heard her say, "Miss Leena, this is a surprise." I became aware of our friends' silence and Jessica's frown, then her anger, then a smile, then an almost giddy, "That's great news. Oh thank you Miss Leena, I sure do appreciate it." The call ended with a, "We'll see you tomorrow." The three of us watched her slowly hang up the phone, drift away momentarily to some unknown mental landscape, only to compose herself as she returned to the present.

"That was Miss Leena, which I guess you knew. It was a classic good-news, bad news case. The bad news was that Frank and Arlene Crawford suddenly appeared. Miss Leena said it was like watching the designated crier at a funeral, so overly emotional and concerned that it was sickening. They created a big scene, talked to Miss Leena for a while, then left."

At that point, Jessica filled in Amy and Derek about the emergence of the woodwork dwellers, and her fears about losing Donna Jo. We discussed that for a short time before I asked about the good news.

Her entire disposition changed. "Miss Leena said that, an hour after the Crawfords left, Donna Jo opened her eyes. That was it. No other response, she just opened her eyes. But Miss Leena said she seemed alert, almost happy. She keeps opening her eyes for a few minutes, then drifting away, then opening her eyes."

"So we're leaving in the morning?"

"Yes."

My wife was animated when she was talking about Donna Jo, in stark contrast to her annoyance and anger when she mentioned the Crawfords. For a moment, we sat quietly, absorbing the news. It was Derek who ended the reverie. "I swear, sometimes I just don't understand people. Sometimes they don't have the common sense that God gave a goat. And you, Jessica, not teaching to be with that poor child. It just makes me so dad gum mad."

Dad gum was about as close to cussing as Derek got. That and dad gums' first cousin, golly bum. I was about to tell him that there was no reason to talk so dirty, but I decided against it.

Jessica repeated all that Theresa had told us. Then she poured herself a big glass of wine and urged us to celebrate the night and each other, and leave the negative news until another time, which is exactly what we did.

It was therapy. For a few hours there was no Cincinnati, no burn unit, no looming legal battle. There was music and laughter, and beer and wine. There was comfort, comfort in knowing that your friends are there for you, with you, by you.

It was after midnight when Amy, the least of the imbibers that evening, drove Derek home. Jessica headed toward the sink, apparently to pour out what was left of her wine. I was incredulous. "What are you doing?"

"What's it look like I'm doing?"

"You can not dump that glass of wine."

"Why not?"

"Because there are people sober in Afghanistan."

"What?"

"Because there are people sober in Afghanistan. You know, it's the adult liquor equivalent of people starving in China, or Africa, or where ever they were starving when you were a kid. It's terrible to waste things when others would love to have it."

"Adam Donahue that may be the dumbest thing you have ever said."

"I'm hurt. Besides, you know that's not true. I've said many dumber things than that. Why, just yesterday ..."

"Forget it." With that, Jessica held up the glass, as if to toast me, then tipped her head back and drained the glass, placing it firmly on the counter to emphasize her completion of the task. "There. I hope that makes you happy. I'm sure that did as much for the Afghanis as eating my vegetables did for the Chinese."

"On behalf of Afghani people everywhere, I thank you."

It was the kind of playful banter I had been missing. I knew she had missed it too, because she was giggling in a wine-induced, sexy way. She washed her glass and leaned against me before taking my hand and leading me to the bedroom, where we made our wonderful evening more wonderful. The last thing I heard was, "Sober in Afghanistan. Give me a break."

I wonder how many nights we actually fall asleep smiling. Whatever the number, I know it's not enough.

CHAPTER 20

The Storm

Or: Getting Uppity

I was slightly hung-over for the drive to Cincinnati. I know that sounds about as logical as being almost pregnant, but in this case, it was true. I didn't have the queasy stomach or the pounding head, but I did have the "cotton mouth" and the eyes that screamed for a gallon of eye drops. Not that I would admit any of this to my spouse as I began the, by now, all too familiar trek toward the Ohio River. I had a strong suspicion that my wife was in the same condition, not that she would ever admit it. It seems that the only thing dumber than talking about sober people in Afghanistan is taking a drink because of it. It seemed so logical in the hot darkness of evening, so silly in the cold light of morning. I was beginning to wonder if it was some form of peer pressure. Could there be peer pressure for middle-age people? Even between husbands and wives? I wanted to think about that, but I got sidetracked, or backtracked, although not front-tracked, by a depressing thought. It had to do with my perception of myself as middle-aged. It is true, I am middle-aged, if I expect to live to be 86. I would have let the depression lead to genuine pissed-offedness, if my wife had not murmured, "I really did have a good time last night."

"I know you did. I did, too. You deserved it." Suddenly, all pissed-offedness evaporated, which is a curious choice of words, even for me.

It started raining half way to Cincinnati. By the time we got there, I was a taunt guitar string, ready to snap. My hands were tense from gripping the wheel, my back and eyes were strained from my leaning slightly forward, doing my best squinting in hopes of increasing visibility. The Tennessee rain had been gentle. The Kentucky rain was what my wife called a gully-washer. By the time we got to Ohio, I was looking for the nearest ark.

We tried the Tennessee tango, two of us under one not quite big enough umbrella, sloshing, arms around each other, through the downpour and the puddles of the parking lot. My left shoulder and arm were drenched; Jessica's right shoulder and arm were equally soaked. We found our separate restrooms and hand driers, or shoulder driers, before heading to Donna Jo's room.

We were met my Miss Leena, who uttered three of the most beautiful words known to man, or woman. "She is awake." My heart and my pace quickened as I followed Miss Leena and Jessica to Donna Jo's bed.

She was only five, so she wasn't exactly huge to begin with, yet each time I saw her, I always seemed surprised by how small she looked. This time was no exception. Yet as I stood there, once again familiarizing myself with the wires and the tubes and the monitors, some new image bombarded my senses. I realized that I had never seen Donna Jo's eyes. Now they were before me, big and brown and beautiful. I had heard people talk about eyes that smiled. I had heard people speak about eyes that danced. Until I saw Donna Jo's eyes focus on Jessica, I always thought it was some figurative, romantic notion. I now believe it happens. Donna Jo's eyes smiled and danced and shouted, "I love you" when she first spied my wife. And Jessica's eyes matched her young student, as I stood, speechless for perhaps the first time in my life. In that quiet moment, I saw, more clearly than I had ever seen anything, the purest and sincerest form of love. I hoped that my eyes were dancing and smiling, although they would have had to do so underwater.

Donna Jo didn't speak, although it appeared that she was trying to. She was able to blink yes and no answers, so there was a conversation. She blinked that she remembered whom I was, that she was in pain, that she knew where she was, that she didn't remember the fire.

We had been there about an hour when Miss Leena returned. She was carrying this glop of goo that looked like part pudding, part cream of wheat, part wallpaper paste. In her best nursing voice, she informed us that, "Miss Donna Jo has not tried solid food for a long time, and it is now time to do so. Maybe Miss Jessica would like to do the honors," and Jessica did exactly that, as though she had fed five-year-old burn victims all her life. It was as natural as breathing, and once again I hoped my eyes were smiling and dancing. Once again, they would have had to do so underwater.

I have no idea how long we stayed. I have no idea why this moved me so deeply. I do remember realizing that I was starving and Donna Jo looked tired and that we should leave. After Jessica said good-bye, I looked directly into Donna Jo's eyes, and said, "Good-bye for now, my brave little princess." It wasn't as natural as breathing, but it didn't seem especially forced or awkward, either. I noticed the watery glistening of Jessica's eyes, and the innocent wonder in our favorite patient's eyes, as we silently made our exit.

We had just left the room when we encountered two people walking toward us. He had a crew cut and a scowl, with thick glasses and dirty shoes, dirty jeans, and dirty hands. He was one of those short, squirrely-looking guys who somehow managed to stick out his chest and saunter like some rooster looking for a henhouse. He was the cock of the walk with no apparent reason for being one. His equally squirrely wife had the opposite persona, like maybe she had been put in her place one time too many. She gave new meaning to the phrase, "dirty blonde," from the stringy hair to the dentist-deprived teeth. I knew, and I knew that Jessica knew, that we were standing in front of Frank and Arlene Crawford.

Old rooster chest stood in our path, sneering. We were about to discover that the Crawfords' physical features would be their most positive characteristics. "Well, look here. I bet it's the Don … a … hues." It was almost like he was spitting out our name, pronouncing each syllable like it was a loathsome, venomous word, ending with extra stress on the last syllable. I detected the smell of alcohol. I don't mind admitting that there is something disconcerting about a stranger not only knowing your name, but hating it. It was a pre-first impression on their part, and a less than stellar beginning on ours. The thought actually crossed my mind, momentarily, that I should smile and extend my hand and be as cordial as Crawford was confrontational. But just as my hand started to move and my mouth started to open, his crowing continued. "Just who da hell ya'll think you are? Sticking your noses in what ain't none of yur business."

I spoke very calmly as I tried to suggest that maybe this wasn't the best place to argue, that we could discuss things rationally, that we all cared about Donna Jo and her welfare. I didn't get very far.

"Lord a mercy, Arlene, you hear that? What they said is true. They are Yankees, hun, damn Yankees tryin' ta meddle in our lives. I ask you again, just who da hell you think you are?"

The next time I'm channel surfing and I come across one of those nature shows that is talking about the momma bear and how she protects her cubs, I will stop and watch and think of my wife. I was about to answer old cow's ass, but momma bear beat me to it. She left no doubt about her Southerness, speaking in her sternest teacher voice. "Who do I *think* I am? I *am* Mrs. Jessica Donahue. I *am* Donna Jo's teacher. I *am*, with the exception of my husband, the only person to visit this child until last weekend." She paused for affect before adding, "And I *am* going to continue."

A smarter man would have backed down immediately. Crawford didn't fit that category. He lit into me. "Well, ain't that sompthin'. You always let yur uppity wife fight yur battles? Maybe ya'll won't be so high and mighty when I slap a retainin' order on ya. Whatcha think a them apples, teacher?"

He stepped one step closer, which was one step too many. I always hated the testosterone-laden, macho crap. I hadn't had a fight since sixth grade. I always thought it was a sign of weakness. Yet here I was, facing a total stranger, and the adrenaline was pumping. It was time to puff out my chest, to become a bigger rooster. I simply said, "No."

"No. No what?"

In my best imitation of a Tennessee senator, I drawled, "No, I don't always let my wife fight my battles. I do all the heavy liftin'. I just let her handle the light stuff. Now, if you fine folks will excuse us, I believe we have had enough bullshit for one day." I was tempted to explain the difference between retaining and restraining, but I didn't. I took my sweet time about leaving, calmly taking my wife's hand. It took Crawford a moment to think of a response, and I suspect he was about to shout something witty at our backs, but I heard Miss Leena setting him straight. Apparently, she had heard some of the exchange, and she wasn't about to put up with any inappropriate activity, not in *her* hospital.

By the time we sloshed back to the car, we were experiencing post idiotic situation stressful encounter disorder. PISSED for short. It was like we had avoided the near fatal car-wreck, now we were feeling the nervousness that comes after the fact.

"So what now?"

"I don't know, maybe we should think about those sober Afghanis."

"Very funny. Adam, do you think they'll try to get a restraining order? I don't think I could accept the idea of those two seeing Donna Jo while you and I can not."

"I know. I'm guessing it's a bluff. I don't think he's got any legal basis for one, but let's call Theresa and see what she says."

Most of the time, I tolerate the fax, pager, cell phone world we live in. Jessica absolutely hates it, but here was one time when both of us were grateful for the cell phone.

Theresa was everything we wanted our lawyer to be. She shared our disgust and anger, sympathized with our concern, and greatly eased our fears, especially when she said, "The Crawfords are the type who receive restraining orders, not initiate them. They are the restrainees, not the restrainers. Don't worry about it." The moment I heard her use the word restrainee, I knew we were in good hands.

"I think we should make one more call."

"Let me guess. Miss Leena."

I love it when my wife and I are on the same wavelength, and I told her so. My actual wavelength is about six feet. Miss Leena had given us her cell phone number. She assured us that very few people had it. It was one of the many gestures that made us respect this special woman. Most of the time her cell phone was off, so as not to disturb her patients, but we left a message. Twenty minutes later, she returned our call.

"They're gone." She knew that was our first concern.

"Do you think they're coming back?"

"They said they were heading home."

"What happened when we left?"

"They started to complain about you. I told them I wasn't interested. He told me not to get uppity with him. Of course, I know he really wanted to call me an uppity you know what, but, he didn't, not when I told him that visiting hours were about to be over. He told me I couldn't do that, I assured him I could, I would, and security was on its way. Suddenly, the bully was much better behaved, especially when too large officers with my skin color strolled in and asked if everything was okay. I told them to stay tuned; I'd let them know. I also told them if I found out that they bothered you, or you suddenly couldn't visit, I'd become their worst nightmare. I think we understood each other."

For the first time since the confrontation, we laughed. We laughed at the fact that Jessica and Miss Leena were both considered uppity. We laughed because two women, one white and one black had stood up to the rooster. We bet that deep down inside, the rooster's wife was loving it. Not that she'd dare to say so. I think we also laughed out of relief. Maybe Miss Leena would have more clout than our lawyer.

Still, we didn't sleep easily that night. The possibility that Donna Jo could end up with Frank and Arlene Crawford haunted us, and would continue to do so as we drove back to Knoxville the next day.

CHAPTER 21

Theresa

Or: Showing Restraint

"The good news is that Donna Jo's neighbors, Ernie Lee and Janie Lowe, have withdrawn their custody petition." It was Theresa, giving us what was becoming a daily briefing. It was, indeed, good news, even if we never saw them as serious competition. Of course, every good news silver lining has a bad news cloud. I held my breath as Theresa continued. "The bad news is that Mr. Crawford has filed a police report. He is claiming that you threatened him. And he is asking for a restraining order." So much for the restrainer, restrainee argument.

"He's what? That's, that's just ridiculous. Adam didn't threaten him. Of all the …" Jessica was on the other line, and she was livid.

"I know. I'm going to Cincinnati in the morning. I'll get a statement from that nurse you always talk about, Miss Leena, isn't it?"

"Yes."

"Then I'll go pay the Cincinnati police a visit. Don't visit the hospital until you hear from me."

"But Theresa, that's not fair."

"No, it's not. But it's only temporary. I think I can handle this, but give me some time."

The truth was that Jessica had come back to Knoxville with me, and had not planned on going back until the day after tomorrow. It was simply the idea that she might be prevented from seeing Donna Jo, that someone else could decide if and when she could visit that was killing her.

"Theresa … I … I mean … what … what is going on? Are we in trouble?"

"I certainly don't think so. But Jessica?"

"Yeah?"

"You've got to let me do my job. I do know the best way to handle things. Please listen to me. Please trust me."

"I will, and I do. But Theresa?"

"Yeah?"

"You may know the law. You may know the procedures. You don't know how this feels."

There was a long silence. I was beginning to think we had lost the connection. Then I heard a strange voice. It wasn't the strong, authoritative lawyer voice. This was a soft, almost soothing, maternal sound. "That's where you are wrong." There was another pause, as Theresa gathered her composure. "I was twenty-three. My daughter was fourteen months. I had just started law school. My two-and-a-half-year marriage was all but over. I knew the divorce was imminent. I was looking at law school as a single parent."

Again Theresa stopped. It was clear that this was not an easy story for her to tell. It was equally clear that she was determined to tell it. "My husband had to take care of Kaylee on the many nights that I was studying at the law library." The word Kaylee personalized her hurt. It was like her pain traveled through cyberspace, entering my ear and settling in my gut. I heard Jessica inhale sharply. "One night, after a group study session, a couple of us went to a bar. We didn't stay long; most of us were too tired and too broke to actually party. Anyway, this male friend and I were the last to leave. I told him about my marriage, how it was all but over. He put his arm around me, friendly-like. He kissed my forehead and told me he'd be there if I needed to talk. It was harmless. At least, I thought it was." Another long pause, and audible breaths, before, "I was being followed. The detective my husband had hired snapped a photo of the bar, and the hug, and the kiss. All of this happened while we were still legally married.

"My husband also had a much better lawyer than I could afford. I'll spare you all the details. Let's say that my divorce was the best legal training I've ever received. My attorney was incompetent, although it might not have mattered. I was painted as an unfit mother, an ambitious and unfaithful woman who put herself and her career ahead of her child. I lost Kaylee. So you're right. I know the law. I vowed that I would never let another woman suffer the humiliation I have. I studied with a vengeance. But you are wrong to say I don't know how you are feeling. I know in ways that, with my help, you may never have to experience."

By the end of her story, the lawyer voice had returned. I heard my wife apologize, and offer all of the well-intentioned, sympathetic clichés that are the best we can do and not nearly good enough. After Theresa hung up, we called Miss Leena to let her know that Theresa would be coming. Then Jessica and I held each other, like we were holding on to more than just another human being. Some days, holding on is about the best a person can hope for.

The following evening, Theresa called to say she had good news that she wanted to deliver in person. Fortunately, she was only minutes away when she called.

I had spent little time with Theresa. My wife did most of the "in office" stuff. I signed papers and listened in on phone calls. I had viewed her as a lawyer—and I admit that my view of the legal system was somewhat jaded. I may have created my own strange syllogism: The legal system stinks, lawyers are part of the legal system, ergo, all lawyers stink. It had its charm. What it neglected was the human element. Of course, saying "all" about any group is the gateway to close-mindedness. I remember thinking all of those thoughts as our lawyer's brisk stride brought her to our front door. She had been to Cincinnati on our behalf. She was still working for us long after we had finished our dinner. Theresa didn't stink. In fact, I was taken by something I had not noticed before. Our lawyer was a beautiful woman. I don't know why I missed that fact previously. I'm usually most perceptive about that kind of thing. I don't know why I noticed it this time, but I suspect her story about losing her daughter made both of us take a second, closer look.

Jessica offered our guest cheese and crackers and wine, an offer that was readily accepted. Once we were settled, Theresa began her narrative. "First of all, let me tell you that Miss Leena is amazing, and I'm not just talking about her nursing skills. By the time I got there, she had a notarized statement ready for me. With that, she handed us a copy. "It is better than most lawyer-prepared briefs, and it could not be more helpful to our case. You can read it later, but basically it says that you are loving people who have demonstrated that love for Donna Jo. It paints Mr. Crawford as belligerent, and as someone who had been drinking when he, not you, provoked the incident. It's a wonderful document."

We weren't surprised by Miss Leena's help, but we were grateful. We just didn't know, yet, how grateful we needed to be. "There's more. Miss Leena took it upon herself to visit the chief of police, one LaMarcus J. Mitchell. If I would have known she was going to do this, I would have told her not to. Usually, that kind of thing is a terrible move. In this case, I'm glad I didn't know. I don't mind telling you that I did not like the attitude I sensed on the phone yesterday. I thought we were in trouble."

"But you said …" That was as far as I got.

"I said you needed to let me do my job. I did it. I just didn't know I was going to have so much help. Anyway, Miss Leena visits the chief, she leaves him a copy of her statement, and by the time I go in to his office, it's like I'm talking to a different person. He could not have been more polite."

"So what about the restraining order?"

Theresa smiled. "The chief handled this part himself. He called Mr. Crawford at work. He works at Home Depot. I'm not sure exactly what he does there, but he was not the least bit happy about being called at his job, not that the chief cared. He told Crawford he was following up on his complaint and wanted to ask a few questions. Crawford got real defensive, and then refused to talk. Said he'd call back when he got off work. So then Mitchell called Mrs. Crawford. He reached her at home. Apparently, she works part-time at a convenience store.

"At first, the chief thought she was going to be less talkative than her husband, but he kept asking questions, and finally she started talking. She admitted that her husband started everything then begged him not to tell her husband she said so. She also indicated that she had no idea when they would get back to Cincinnati. 'It costs a lot of money, ya know?' The more she talked, the clearer things became. I'm not sure she really wants Donna Jo. I think it's all her husband's idea, and she isn't going to stand up to him. They clearly don't have much money. I'm not sure what they're thinking.

Anyway, by the time the chief was done, he knew the truth. There is no restraining order. He said he'd just wait on Mr. Crawford's call, and in the unlikely event that he did call, the chief was sure he might be in a meeting or out of the office or working on the Jimmy Hoffa case. You are free to visit any time you want, and I doubt if you'll see the Crawfords if you do."

We could not have felt more relieved, but Theresa gave us one more reminder of why she was more than our lawyer. "I want to tell you one more thing. When I was done talking to Miss Leena about the incident, I asked her if I could see Donna Jo. She took me to see her. Her skin looks so painful. She is swollen and black in some places, blistered and pink in others. Yet she is still beautiful. Miss Leena says she's a fighter; that she might not have survived without that spirit. While we stood there, watching her sleep, Miss Leena whispered, 'You just got to make this work out right. Don't let those Crawford folks get this little girl.' I promised her, and I promise you, that I won't let it happen."

Theresa stayed for a second glass of wine. We talked about the adoption, and the Shriners, and all that faced Donna Jo. After she left, Jessica and I continued to speculate. Neither of us was tired. Neither of us was prepared for what was ahead.

CHAPTER 22

Bobble Heads Revisited

Or: Close Enough

"All eyes were on me. It felt disgusting, so I threw them off."

Jessica had fired the first volley. It had been a while, but here we were, driving to Cincinnati, and she had started the game. I didn't know if the category was body parts or literal language, but I was ready for the challenge. "I had a leg up on my competition, but it was not comfortable."

"In a dog-eat-dog world, who gets the last bite?"

"When you dog-ear a page of a book, does it hear sounds you can't?"

"Does it hurt when you get kicked out of something?"

"Does it hurt when you have a lot on your mind?"

"What pumps the blood when your heart is on your sleeve?"

"How can you drive if your head is up your …?"

"Stop. Foul. Adam, do you always have to get crude?"

"What, throwing off squishy eyeballs isn't crude?"

"You know what I mean. You always want to go to the lowest common bathroom denominator."

"And you get to decide what's too crude?"

"Yes. I think somebody needs to, and clearly you are not capable."

"So a pecker-head reference would be outlawed as well?"

"Of course."

"Fine. Just as long as I know the new and improved rules, as amended and interpreted by you."

"Exactly."

"Then I withdraw my last offering. I'll turn the other cheek, so to speak, and ask, 'If the shoe's on the other foot, where's the other shoe? Do they only have one?"

"Why don't we ever hear about outgrown toenails? Why do the ingrown toenails get all the attention?"

"If you outgrow a toenail what do you do with it? Does it become a hand-me-down? Or a toe-me-down?"

Most games never really end. They fizzle. Somebody get tired, the game gets ridiculous, the subject gets changed, and it's over. Then both of us claim victory. Today's contest seemed destined for the same fate, but instead of a fizzle, this one came to a dramatic end. About a mile up the road, a min-van went to change lanes. Apparently, the driver of the van did not realize he was changing to a lane that was already occupied by a small pickup truck. The truck veered right, seemed to be riding on two wheels as it prepared to flip over; then somehow righted itself on all four wheels as it reached the shoulder of the highway. Somehow, the driver kept the truck from running off the road, finally stopping his vehicle hundreds of yards past the point of contact. There was no sign of the van. We pulled over to check on the driver, who was shaken but fine. The truck was damaged, but drivable. He thanked us for our concern, but we really were of no help. I described the van to him, but I had no license number.

The truck driver called the police, but they weren't very helpful. By the time we all returned to driving the interstate, we were shaken and relieved, upset and grateful, anxious and alert. It was another one of those graphic reminders of how quickly things can change, and how fragile life can be. We spent the next few miles talking about what might have been and cussing the idiot in the van who just took off. By the time we got to the hospital, the incident was relegated to that place in our minds that files or sublimates the nearly traumatic. I did not think it appropriate to ask what happens if the road's shoulder shrugs, although it did cross the median in my mind. I'm glad I didn't mention it. It would not have helped what we were about to face.

CHAPTER 23

Burns

Or: Skin Deep

Sometimes I wonder about my listening skills. Jessica had talked to the doctors, had studied the internet, and told me all about Donna Jo's medical problems. I know she did. I know I heard the words, but I also know I could not repeat any of them. Now, we were meeting with Dr. Henri Thakkurian, a small man with a firm handshake and a large smile. Miss Leena introduced us, and remained with us in the small conference room that was just down the hall from the burn unit. Dr. Thakkurian spoke with a British accent, a sharp contrast to the black hair and dark skin of his native India. He seemed obligated to quickly explain that he left his native land when he was four, going with his father, the college professor, and his mother, the physical therapist, to London, where he remained until his graduation from college. He was accepted at Duke University Med School, and had been at the Shriners Hospital since completing his residency.

With the preliminaries out of the way, the doctor began a review of all that had been done and all that remained. At least it was a review for Miss Leena and Jessica. "First, let me say that dehydration is no longer a concern. The wraps on her feet and legs have done their job. Most of the burns there are superficial. She had two second-degree burns on her left thigh, but those have healed. I'd say the lower region had responded quite nicely."

I would have enjoyed the accent and the "quite nicely" much more if it didn't sound as if one big "but ..." were coming, which of course is exactly what was coming.

"I'm concerned about her upper back and shoulders. Those areas are larger, slightly deeper, and more difficult to heal. Still, I don't think invasive procedures will be required."

I asked about the meaning of invasive procedures, got an explanation from the doctor and an "I can't believe you asked that when I've told you all of this" look from my wife. I tried to recover with an, "Oh, right, you've mentioned this," but I'm not sure Jessica was buying it. If I'd only kept my mouth shut, I would have learned all about the procedures anyway, because that was the next area to be addressed.

"It's time to begin the hard part. She has several areas I want to address immediately. The first is the area from her left elbow to the top of her shoulder. That will require the use of dermal regeneration templates."

I had been impressed with how un-technical the language had been. I should have known that the medical lingo would appear at some point. I wondered if I was supposed to know about this, too. I was debating whether I should ask, and risk further evidence of my listening ineptness, or remain silent, and clueless. Jessica came to my rescue. "Doctor, could you review that process, please?" I noticed that she looked at me when she asked, but I swear it looked like she was fighting a smile.

"Sure. We will apply a silicone template to the damaged skin. It works as a stimulus of sorts. It acts like skin temporarily, but it encourages the skin cells to rejuvenate, to grow new skin. Eventually, the template biodegrades, and the new skin takes its place. It is less invasive and produces less scarring than the alternative."

I wanted to shout, "You can do that? You can create this artificial skin-like stuff and magically produce new skin?" Somehow, I suspected that wouldn't win any points, so I quietly asked, "The alternative?"

"Skin grafts." I could tell I was supposed to know this, and as he said it I knew that I had been in a discussion about it. Maybe it had all seemed so distant or theoretical before. I suddenly wanted to catch up, to know at least as much as Jessica did about what Donna Jo was going through.

Dr. Thakkurian had paused, as if knowing I needed to process all of this, before he continued, "Donna Jo's worst burns are on the left side of her face and neck. I wish we could use dermal regenerative templates there, but we can't. We need to do skin grafts, some split thickness grafts, some full thickness grafts. This is where it gets risky."

For the next few minutes, my listening skills were exemplary. I learned about the various layers of the skin, and what it means to damage each one. I learned about the risk of infection, about plastic surgery and the importance of therapy in the recovery process. I learned about donor sites, the area from which the healthy skin is harvested, and how that area would have its own problems to address. By the time I understood all that a non-medical person was capable of understanding, by the time I was getting use to all the procedures that were going to be visited on such a young child, another issue surfaced.

Surfaced was the right word, because the issue had always been there, swimming below the surface. It was the issue of what rights we had, if any, in this entire process. The doctor had no reason to talk to us. We had no legal standing to make any decisions about her treatment. Actually, we discovered later, the doctor did have one reason to talk to us. That reason was named Miss Leena. I don't know what she did to convince him, but I was glad that she did it.

After the doctor left, a disconcerted Miss Leena said, "The Department of Children's Services is involved. They say we have to deal with the relatives in this case. We need to sit down with the Crawford's and tell them what we've told you. They are the only people who can authorize the procedures. If the Crawford's don't, then the agency can act on the child's behalf. You can't do anything unless you have custody. So, ah, let's keep this meeting to ourselves. And let's see if this legal mumbo-jumbo can be fixed, 'cause the idea of dealing with those two relatives of Donna Jo's? I'd rather you just beat me with a two by four."

I looked at Donna Jo differently when we saw her. I tried to picture her after the procedures. Would she be scarred? I knew her color would change, but what about her features? How much pain would she feel? What if the grafts didn't take? That was Dr. Thakkurian's way of describing an unsuccessful procedure. What if there was infection? It seemed that we had been going to Cincinnati for years, even though it had only been months. Now it seemed that there was more ahead of us than behind us.

Donna Jo was a statistic, a casualty to the epidemic that is methamphetamine. She never asked for this. I thought I had buried the resentment I felt for her parents. For the most part, I had, but it reappeared as I studied their daughter. The survivor. Eventually, that resentment was replaced by a more positive emotion. I realized how grateful I was for all of the cosmic twists and turns that had to happen for Dr. Henri Thakkurian and Donna Jo Crawford to be written into the same story. I also realized it was up to Theresa to make that story have a happy ending.

Faith

Or: Deep Purple

"I left my church. I'm hoping to find another one."

Jessica had resumed her weeklong visits to Cincinnati, and I was spending another Thursday with Derek and Amy. In light of our past religious discussions, I was surprised that Derek was initiating the conversation, but more surprised with his comment. I knew he wanted a friend who would listen, and I wanted to be that friend. I hoped my, "Why" was sufficient.

"*The Color Purple*."

"*The Color Purple*?"

"Yup. *The Color Purple*."

"You mean the book, not the shade, right?"

He nodded. Alice Walker's novel was almost ten years old. I'd read the book, and enjoyed it. I knew that Derek had, also. I also knew there was some controversy, which helped sales. I couldn't believe it would be a part of Derek leaving a church to which he had been so loyal.

"Let me start over. To understand my problem, you have to know that Amy stopped going months ago. We didn't mention it because, well, religious issues aren't always our best topics for discussions."

I started to protest, knew I shouldn't, and settled for asking if Alice Walker had caused her defection as well.

Amy entered the conversation. "No. I quit over subserviency." When she correctly sensed that I had no idea what she was talking about, she elaborated.

"The Southern Baptist Convention has decided that our country is going to hell. Again. This is not new; it has almost always been going to hell. What is new this time is the cause. One of the major reasons for our hell bound condition is our society's abandonment of traditional roles. Our church, our former church, has embraced this call for traditional family values. Our preacher actually delivered a sermon demanding that women be subservient to men. That, according to him, is the way the Bible demanded things should be. I left that day, and to be perfectly honest, I was mad and hurt and disappointed that Derek didn't quit then, also."

It was Derek's turn to explain. "I understood Amy's point. I didn't get as upset because, well, first of all, I never wanted Amy to be subservient. She's been my partner, my equal, in all that we've done. She's been a wonderful wife and mother and an outstanding nurse. She makes more money than I do. It's never been an issue. So I just figured it was one of those areas where I disagreed with the church. Those things happen."

I remembered my own Catholic upbringing. The most devout followers I knew didn't practice all that the church preached. I didn't know anyone who agreed with the Pope's ban of all forms of birth control except the unreliable rhythm method. Yet all of those people would have gladly kissed the Pope's ring if given the opportunity. "So you went to church alone?"

"Not for long. Shortly after Amy's departure, I had my own problem. I drove by the church after school one day, and I read the topic for the upcoming sermon. It was, 'Purple—The Color of Evil.' I thought it was some sort of joke, or sarcasm, or some clever attention getter that really wasn't what it seemed to be. So I called our preacher. It wasn't a joke, and it wasn't the least bit clever. The book had been assigned to a student in our congregation. Even though he hadn't read the book, he'd seen enough excerpts and heard enough about it to know it was not something our children should read. I guess the English teacher in me couldn't take the censorship. I started to argue, but I knew it was pointless. I politely hung up, and I haven't been back since."

I didn't know what to say. "I'm not surprised" somehow didn't seem right. Neither did, "What did you expect?" As I fumbled for a response, Amy rescued me. "Tell him the rest of it."

"It's not important."

"I think it is. Go on, tell him."

Derek sighed, telling the story in much the same manner as a student would tell the principal why he had been sent to the office. "I hate this part. I said it's not important, because I want to believe that, but maybe it is important. At first, whenever I saw anyone from church, I got the typical, 'we missed you last Sunday.' Of course we all know they aren't talking about missing someone so much as they are asking for a reason for not attending. It is polite, Southern interrogation. I didn't want to lie, so I told the truth. It didn't take long for, well, for me to become an outcast."

I had heard about this kind of treatment, but had never actually witnessed it. I passed it off as exaggeration. Certainly it did not still occur, not in our kinder, gentler, modern society. "What do you mean by an outcast?"

"I mean outcast, pariah, persona non grata. Let's just say that the Amish aren't the only ones versed in shaming and shunning. The few church members who still actually speak to me are curt and cool. There are some who ignore me, who won't make eye contact, who leave if I enter a room. I teach with some of those people. Twice I've seen people cross the street to avoid passing me on the sidewalk. Even some of my students acted differently at first. I thought, or hoped, that I was imagining all this, but I'm not. Amy's seen it, although not at her work."

We spent the next hour talking about Alice Walker and subservient women and literal interpretations of the Bible and unchristian acts of supposedly Christian people. We might have talked for another hour if Jessica hadn't called. She called because Donna Jo was awake and more alert than she had been during previous awakenings. She called because she missed me and wanted me to share in that good news. But most of all, she called because Theresa had been unable to find me. We had a date for the custody hearing, and it was next week.

Jessica's news ended our theological discussion, at least momentarily. I allowed myself to be caught up in the thrill of anticipation and the joy of an improving patient. Amy fought back tears as we discussed the potential resolution; the resolution that would make my wife the mother she longed to be, and me the father I hoped to be.

As I was leaving, Derek thanked me for listening, for caring, and most of all for not gloating. I told him there was nothing to gloat about, that I was genuinely sorry for what he had been through. He responded, "But you aren't the least bit surprised, are you?"

"I'm surprised it happened to you, because you were always so sure of your faith, but otherwise, no, I'm not surprised."

"Adam, I'm still sure of my faith. That hasn't changed."

I was touched by the simple sincerity of his statement. He ended the evening by wishing me good luck with the hearing, not that he thought I needed it. His last words were, "I'll be praying for you."

I thanked him. Driving home, I couldn't help thinking about how different my best friend and I are. Derek's experience only increased my cynicism. Somehow, even though he had lost faith in his church, his strength and deep personal, spiritual faith remained strong, in fact, was strengthened by the ordeal. I respected that, perhaps even envied it.

CHAPTER 25

Judgment Day

Or: I'll Be a Cow's Ass

We owed no money to anyone. We had paid off our twenty-year mortgage in fifteen years. Both of our parents, when they died, left us small amounts of money. For most of our married lives, both of us worked. We had no children. We were able to save a significant sum of money. We were not rich, but we were quite comfortable.

It seemed that we saved for trips we never took, home improvements we never started, and a retirement we did not want. We complained about our jobs but enjoyed working. We were confident that our financial situation and Jessica's willingness to stay at home with Donna Jo were our strengths, especially since we were well educated. Jessica's obvious show of concern at the hospital was, perhaps, the most compelling indication of her love for the girl who was at the center of the hearing.

The Crawfords lived from paycheck to paycheck. They had mortgages and liens and credit card debt that might never be paid. She was a high school graduate; he had a G.E.D. I caught myself beginning to feel sorry for them, and that made me disgusted with myself. Was my pity a form of some smug, superior attitude on my part? Was I looking down on them because of social status? Or was I doing so because I knew, more certainly than I knew my own name, that Donna Jo would be better served living with us?

Frank and Arlene had cleaned up nicely. In fact, they both looked a decade younger than they had the first time I saw them. Even then, they still looked older than they were. I was shocked to find that he was thirty-one. She was twenty-eight. Their youth was a positive factor for them, one their lawyer kept repeating.

I'm not sure what I expected. I know I didn't anticipate a crusty old judge who seemed to have no patience, yet allowed the proceeding to drag on at the speed of a caterpillar turning into a butterfly. That includes the birth of the caterpillar, its maturing to a cocoon builder, and it emergence all those months later. Glaciers moved faster than old Judge Clayborne. Over numerous objections by Theresa, he allowed questions to be asked and re-asked and answered and re-answered. I felt like I was in the middle of some judicial filibuster.

Somehow, the Crawfords had hired a bright, young lawyer. From the moment ol' Davis Richardson III opened his mouth, I knew Theresa had her hands full. He had that oh shucks, I'm just a simple, good-ol' country boy attitude that oozed friendliness while you just knew he was plotting your castration. I didn't care much for Mr. Richardson.

We trudged through the Crawford history. They were young, planned on having children in the near future, no matter how this case turned out. They didn't visit Donna Jo because they couldn't afford it. It isn't easy for "workin' folk" to just "up and go ta Cincinnati." A moment later they assured the court they could support a new child. They loved Donna Jo. Used to visit all the time before the accident. Warned her parents about that meth. Didn't know they were cookin' it right there. Thought they'd given it up. Wanted to do the right thing, be good kinfolk, just knew it was their duty to raise this child. After all, they were her only relations in the entire world.

Like a C.D. in the repeat mode, that theme repeated itself to the point of annoyance. By then, even Clayborne was tired, so he adjourned until the next morning.

Theresa remained optimistic, but I suspected that was for our benefit. I never really understood the phrase "loose cannon" until I sat in Judge Clayborne's courtroom. Although he didn't seem to have the firepower (or brain power) of a cannon, he was so loose I expected the one remaining screw to pop out at any moment. He would be an unhinged B.B. gun, but even those can do damage.

The Crawfords were given an opportunity to finish anything they hadn't addressed yesterday. There was one well-rehearsed grand finale from Frank Crawford. "We may not be as rich as them folks," he was pointing at us the way a gardener would point out a cutworm, "but just cause a body has money don't make 'em better 'n us. I'm a good Christian man, and my wife is a good Christian woman, and I just wanta know one thing. What church you belong to? What church will Donna Jo belong to? Do you read the Bible? Cause I knowed her mommy and daddy, and they made mistakes, and got caught up in that meth, but they always wanted their daughter to be brought up in the church. Your honor, I'll see to it that their wishes are met."

We were prepared for the religious questions. We were prepared for Theresa's objections to be overruled. We were not prepared for the effect our answers would have. No, we were not atheists. No, we didn't go to church. Yes, we thought it was important for a child to go. Yes, we would see to it that she went. At one point, as I tried to explain how I felt it was a personal decision, I swore I saw the judge roll his eyes. Jessica got caught up trying to explain that she wouldn't be a bad role model if she allowed Donna Jo to try different churches while she herself went to none. At that point, I know Davis Richardson III rolled his eyes, and again I thought the judge did, also.

I had one final bad moment to endure. We had, to the best of our ability to do so, listed all of the days that Jessica had spent at the hospital. We thought it demonstrated how dedicated she was to Donna Jo. Suddenly, I found that fact being thrown back at me. It was clearly a sign of a poor marriage if we chose to spend so much time apart. Loving couples, like the Crawfords, did not go for days on end separated like that. It wasn't normal. Maybe Jessica preferred the hospital and a comatose girl to her own husband. Once again, Theresa's objections could not stop the absurdity that was being allowed in court. I decided to object on my own. "Mr. Richardson, I resent your totally false characterization of the most important thing I have—my marriage. You don't know a thing about it, sir, and I do not appreciate your accusations. I love my wife enough to sacrifice our short term time together for a greater good—a long term commitment that hopefully involves the child she has agonized over since this tragedy occurred."

If I had stopped there I might have made a difference, although I doubt it. I actually had stopped there, but Davis Richardson III, in his most condescending tone and manner, erupted, "Really. What a touching story. It's about the sacrifice, I see. You sure you didn't have other extracurricular activities planned?"

Even Judge Clayborne knew that crossed some mystical line, and said so while Theresa was objecting. But I could not let it pass, I could not keep my mouth shut at the time it most needed shutting. I had to add, "It is about sacrifice. And love, and if you don't get that, you pompous ass, then you're not as smart as you pretend to be."

It felt great. For all of thirty seconds. That's how long the words hovered there, before sinking in on every person in the courtroom. I watched Jessica lower her head, watched Theresa stare at her notepad, saw the Crawfords smirk, then watched as Richardson struck an actor's pose, pausing for just the right moment before uttering, "Pompous ass. Yes, I'm sure the court would want to put an unrelated child into an environment where that type of language is used."

Theresa did as much damage control as possible. She ripped into her opposing counsel, who maintained a "Who, me?" countenance as she pointed out that there was no indication I would speak that way in front of a child. In fact, I thought for a while that Theresa's final comments just might save the day. The court recessed until the next morning, when Judge Clayborne told us what we all knew was coming.

The Crawfords, as the only living relatives, were the most logical choice for Donna Jo. There was no doubt in the courts mind that they would provide a good, Christian environment, that what they lacked in material possessions would be made up for in love. Davis Richardson III then asked, in an attempt to allow the Crawfords to begin their responsibility smoothly, that we be instructed to stay away from Donna Jo. We were, and court was adjourned.

Theresa said lots of things, none of which I heard. I tried to hold Jessica, but she would not allow it. We rode home in silence, broken only by Jessica's weeping. I think we said some things once we were home, but nothing worth remembering.

I do remember that Derek called. I remember telling him something about his prayers failing, that the Crawfords were clearly morally superior in God's eyes, and that maybe God needed to get his eyes checked. I know we didn't talk long.

The thing I do remember is walking outside, beer in hand, and sitting on the step with Atticus. I remember thinking that Atticus was the perfect companion. I remember realizing that I was grieving for the loss of a child I never had, and perhaps for the loss of a wife I did. I made a vow that that would not happen. Then I buried my face in my dog's fur and cried like the cow's ass I was.

CHAPTER 26

Silence

Or: The Hangover

For three days, Jessica silently sulked, grieving for the death of a child who was still very much alive. The only words she uttered were, "I can't even see her. Can't tell her ..." Her voice would trail off, the sound replaced by sighs that were too choked with tears and too laden with pain to flow smoothly. Her halting, uneven inhalation made her body quiver; her equally quirky exhalation caused her to shake and contort. Then she would be quiet, as if forgetting to breathe, until the next wave washed over her, causing the laborious process to begin again.

She listened to all of my words, nodding slightly but saying nothing. She tolerated my attempts at holding and comforting her, but only momentarily, before finding a reason to pull away.

I understood her pain, or at least I thought I did. I began to resent her lack of empathy. I hurt also, and no one seemed to care. I too had invested my heart and hopes in Donna Jo. I went from fearing fatherhood to embracing it. I had painted those visual images we all paint as we picture the possible, and fantasize our future. I liked that picture. I mourned its loss, and my wife did not seem to care.

Theresa called daily. She wanted to talk about legal options. Neither of us was prepared for that. Amy and Derek called, and even stopped by, but the conversations were brief. I told them to be patient with us, to keep trying, but to understand that we were not ready to talk to them.

I don't know how long we would have maintained that quiet desperation if fate hadn't stepped in. In this case, fate had a name. The name was Miss Leena.

We were sitting, staring, silently brooding. Jessica slowly stood up, went to the closet, pulled on her jacket, and headed outside. For a moment, I thought she might be leaving me, but she was simply going outside. It was her first time out since we arrived home after the trial. I watched as she let Atticus out of the kennel; then headed into the woods. I thought it was healthy. It was at that moment the phone rang.

I considered not answering it, but an incessantly ringing, unanswered phone is one of the most effective torture techniques I know.

Theresa had notified Miss Leena about the verdict, and about the way we were taking it. Miss Leena wanted to talk to both of us. I explained that Jessica was outside, and that we weren't exactly talking, and some other self-indulgent, self-pitying tripe. That's when I got what I deserved, and needed.

"Do you love your wife?"

"Yes, of course, but ..."

"No buts. You got one job to do, you hear me? You got to stop feelin' sorry for yourself. You gonna let this ruin your marriage?"

"I'm not sure she cares about that."

"I thought you were smarter than that."

"No offense, Miss Leena, but you weren't there. You don't know how bad it was, how bad I was, and how badly she is taking it."

"No offense, Mr. Donahue, but I didn't have to be there. Theresa told me. The judge is the bad person here, not you and not your wife. You 'spose to be a team. You gonna be a team or an individual? You gonna be a fighter or a quitter?"

"What if Jessica quits?"

"She won't. Let me tell you something. Your wife just went through labor. Not a typical labor, but a labor just the same. And now, well, she done lost the baby. Only this wasn't no ordinary miscarriage. It was a miscarriage of justice, but it was like a baby miscarriage, only in this case, the mother saw the baby, knew the baby, bonded with the baby. Of course she is in pain. Of course she is withdrawing. Would you want to be married to someone who didn't suffer this way? Who didn't love and hurt this deeply?"

I knew she was right about Jessica. I knew it was up to me, but I wasn't ready to admit that. "She blames me. I wasn't very good in court. And the idea that she can't visit Donna Jo, well ... I ... we thought we would win. It doesn't seem right or fair."

"It is not right or fair. I know that. Theresa knows that. Listen to her. She can help. But first, talk to your wife."

"I will."

"Okay then."

"Have they been there?"

"The Crawfords?"

"Yeah."

There was a pause, an "I don't exactly know how to say this" kind of pause, and a sigh, and then "Yeah. They were here. Sashayed in like they was somethin' special. Started talkin' 'bout moving her home. Got into an argument with the doctor, who is not about to discharge that child till she is ready. They said they were not going to allow the skin grafts. Said it was just to make someone look good. Doctor tried to explain it wasn't just for looks, but you can't reason with a stubborn old fool."

It was then, at that exact moment, when I knew how to approach Jessica. When the focus of my conversation with Miss Leena turned to Donna Jo, I felt differently. I knew my wife would also. We talked about her progress. She was awake and speaking most of the time now. She had asked about us, both of us. I tried to tell my favorite nurse how much her call had meant to me, and hopefully to Jessica. She said it was all in the day's work, and wished me well.

It was a long time before Jessica came in. She hung up her jacket, clearly intent on continuing her silent grieving.

"The Crawfords don't want the skin grafts."

"What?"

"I said ..."

"Yeah. I heard what you said. I meant what are you ... they can't ... how do you know?"

"Miss Leena called while you were outside."

For a moment, I thought she was going to walk away, to continue withdrawing, I think she was giving that strong consideration, but she found a way to stay, to respond with a less than encouraging, "Oh."

"She says we need to talk to Theresa. There may be ..."

"Screw Theresa. Screw the legal system, and screw you. I cannot go through any more of this. Besides, you'll only cuss out a lawyer or do something stupid."

"So you are blaming me?"

"Yes. Mr. pompous ass, I'm blaming you and our incompetent attorney and our shit-for-brains judge and that scumbag lawyer and, and ..."

She was crying again, trying to catch her breath and make sense at the same time. She stood, fists clenched, as angry as I had ever seen her. She glared at me, as if she wanted to strike me, as if I were her most loathsome enemy.

I wanted to scream back, but I found myself doing the opposite. As quietly as I could, in not much more than a whisper, I asked, "Do you want me to leave? Do you want me out of your life forever? Because if you do, I love you enough to do that. But I don't think it will help. And it would kill me." Now I was crying, and having trouble breathing. But I knew I had to continue. "I am so very, very sorry about the hearing. I got baited, sucked in. He is a pompous ass, but I shouldn't have let him get to me. He attacked you, our marriage, what I love most. Maybe he was right. Maybe our marriage isn't as strong as I thought."

"Adam ... I ... please don't ..."

"Jessica, we didn't lose Donna Jo because of me. I admit that I didn't help, but they were *family*. Church going family, and if I had been a perfect gentleman, we were going to lose. But we're supposed to be a team. We should never let someone or something divide us. Please, Jessica. I don't want to lose you."

Her tears were different now, streaming down her cheeks without the accompanying tidal wave of sobs. Slowly, almost cautiously, she walked to me, reaching for my face. She leaned against me, shivering, summoning all of her strength in order to whisper, "I know you weren't the reason we lost." We stood for some time. She allowed me to lead her to the couch, where we sat holding hands.

"I love you, Jessica."

"I love you, too. And I'm sorry for the way I acted."

"I think I understand." I told her what Miss Leena had said. I told her that I would do anything I could to help, just as long as she didn't shut me out.

"I'm a teacher. I ask people to tell me what they are feeling. Yet somehow, I couldn't bring myself to tell you. I was mad at the world, hated the world, hated you; hated me. It must be like some strange post partum depression, without the actual delivery. I never really let myself think about losing, you know? Every time it crossed my mind I shut it out. And never, not one time, did I think that I would be told to stay away from a child."

There were more tears, and more long moments of silence, but there were also periods of communication. We were making up, slowly. We would survive.

CHAPTER 27

Parents

Or: Night of the Living Dread

"Do I have a story for you." Derek was the perfect medicine. We had spent time with Theresa, searching for possible grounds for appeals. She was not optimistic, but she was thorough. I was able to escape into my work, at least during the day. Jessica had, years ago, been an artist. I don't know why she stopped, but she did. I was delighted when I saw her painting again.

Yes, we were able to find escape in the daytime. But at night, when there was no bookstore or no blank canvas to distract us, we were haunted; haunted by what had happened, and haunted by the unknown. Did Donna Jo think we had abandoned her? That we didn't care? Was the doctor going to convince the Crawfords that they had to do the skin grafts? Did she miss us?

"You want to hear it?"

"I'm sorry, what?"

"My story. You want to hear it?"

Amy entered the fray. "You want my husband to cry?"

I pretended to contemplate her question before deciding I would like to hear the story.

"So, the other night, it's parents' night, okay? You know, parents come in, see how their kid is doing, the whole nine yards."

I could not resist. "Why is it always nine yards? Why not ten? Or a hundred?"

"Great question. Anyway, my friend Kevin, the math teacher, he has this mother come in. She's a big woman, and Kevin's all friendly and everything, and he looks at her stomach and says, 'So, when is the baby due?' And she says, 'I'm not pregnant.' And Kevin wants to die, on the spot, so he tries to cover by saying he must have gotten her mixed-up with another mom who was expecting, but he knew it was a bad attempt to cover-up and so did she. He said it was the worst conference he ever had."

I didn't know how Jessica would react to the pregnancy humor, but she seemed fine. Our friends had asked us to join them several times before we accepted. It was good to return to something approaching normal.

Parents' night always proved interesting to Derek. Usually, he met with the parents of the kids who were doing well. The parents of the poor students rarely visited. When they did, it provided an insight into why they were doing poorly. He agonized over those who really had little chance of success, their home lives were that bad. Yet he always had what he preferred to call the "colorful visits," the ones that added a certain flair to the evening. Like the cantankerous father who just stopped in to say, "If my boy gives ya any trouble, let me know so I kin whip his ass," or the mother of the girl who had terrible attendance who said, "I know she misses some days, but sometimes I need her to stay at home and help me. It ain't easy raisin' her eight younger brothers and sisters." Every year he had at least one parent who thought his or her son was going to play pro football, even though he wasn't getting much playing time on his high school team, or one who thought his or her daughter was going to an elite college, even with a report card full of D's and F's. It was truly an educational experience.

I could not help but think about Donna Jo and the Crawfords. What would they be like on parents' night? How come all of those people Derek met got to have kids, and Jessica did not? I'm sure my wife was wondering the same thing. It was Amy who said, "Maybe this isn't the best conversation right now."

Derek immediately apologized, but we both assured him it was fine, which of course it really wasn't, but we weren't going to say that.

Two days later, I awoke to find my wife staring out the window. When I called her name, she slowly turned, trying to brush away the evidence that she had been crying. "I'm sorry. I told myself I wouldn't let this day bother me. It's just, well, it's her birthday. Donna Jo is six today. I wish I could tell her happy birthday."

It was a bad day. Jessica did no painting that day. When I got home from work I found her just sitting, staring. She was still in the bathrobe she had on when I left. She admitted she had not eaten, and I had to coax her to eat the soup and sandwich I fixed. After all of her apparent progress, this felt like a regression. I hoped it was temporary, I feared it wasn't.

Fortunately, my fears were unfounded. The next morning, she seemed fine, almost cheerful. When she started painting again, relief washed over me like a soothing hot shower on a cold winter day, replacing the chill of fear with the warmth of security, and hope. We had survived another chilling day.

CHAPTER 28

Jessica

Or: In the Beginning

It was love at third sight. It's not as romantic as first sight, but it is what happened.

Jessica and I were in Washington, D.C. for Earth Day, actually for the weekend-long celebration of Earth Day. The first time I met her was on the mall, by the Lincoln Memorial. We met, we talked, I thought she was beautiful and interesting and someone I'd never see again, only I did see her again, at breakfast the next morning. That's when I thought she was a snob. Turns out I misread that situation, but I didn't know that at the time. We would have gone our separate ways if I hadn't seen her at breakfast again the following morning. I was beginning to wonder if this was some sort of fate. This time we talked long after we had finished eating. We went to the final rally together, walked around the mall, visiting the museums and the memorials. By then, I knew I loved her. We spent several more days together, both of us postponing our scheduled return trips. On the last night she told me, "I don't think my daddy would like you." It wasn't your standard, romantic line. When I asked why, she responded, "He'll say you're a damn Yankee, and a Catholic Yankee at that. Then he'll say you're a liberal, and he'll accent all three syllables like they're dirty words."

I wasn't sure how to answer that. All I could think of was, "And what will you say?"

"I'll say that it's part of your charm." Then she pressed me about my parents.

"I honestly don't know. I guess they'll be relieved that you aren't black, or Jewish. Those are two negatives in their eyes. You may be okay if we hide the Baptist thing from them."

"And the Southern thing?"

"I honestly don't know. I don't remember them ever talking to or about Southerners."

"That's 'cause people don't migrate to the North."

I hadn't thought of that, nor did it occur to me that we were already talking about meeting each other's parents, which with any other female would have been my cue to run. I didn't run. Instead, we shared wine and dreams. She said, "Tell me something personal, something you don't normally talk about."

I told her about the jellyfish. I told her that it wasn't getting stung that bothered me; it was the fact that I appeared to be the only one oblivious to what seemed to be common knowledge. Then I asked her to tell me her story.

Jessica blushed, but smiled in spite of that. "I came home and told my parents I didn't understand why everyone called me a Virginian when we lived in Tennessee. At first they didn't understand, or maybe they just pretended like they didn't. Anyway, this was in eighth grade, and it seemed like this group of girls had nothing better to do than to point and laugh and call me names. Finally, over Sunday chicken and dumplings, my dad told me they were saying virgin, not Virginian. Mother looked like she was going to pass out, just plop face down into the gravy or something, especially when I told them if being a virgin was so bad I didn't want to be one anymore. I asked what I could do to fix that, and that's when mother actually stood up and announced that this was not appropriate dinner conversation, especially on the Sabbath, and that I should be ashamed. So much for dear old mom's approach to sexual education. A couple of days later I got these absolutely pathetic books about the 'facts of life.' Some church group had thrown them together. I found a couple of other 'Virginians,' and we were able to finally learn the truth. I guess I understand what it's like to be one of the oblivious ones."

We discovered that neither one of us were particularly worldly growing up. I certainly wasn't aware of any eighth grade action, and I was happy she wasn't, either. Both of us were surprised to be telling our embarrassing moments so early on in our relationship, and with such ease. Jessica made me laugh. She also made me willingly overcome that typical male fear of commitment crap. And later that evening, in a surprisingly untypical act for both of us, we shared each other. It was untypical because it happened so early in the relationship, and untypical because it felt so beautiful, so comfortable, so genuine.

The following morning we walked to the bus station. I had never experienced a painful good-bye before. I found the hurt to be wonderful, wonderful because of what it signified. I had someone to hurt about. Just before my bus arrived, she looked into my eyes in a way no one ever has, not before and not after. She said, "Adam Donahue, if you don't keep all of your promises about writing and calling, I swear to you I will convert to your religion and join a bloody convent." Years later, I would remind her of that parting line. We would laugh about the bloody convent, the B.C. as it became known.

I kept those promises, and the vow to love her until I die. After a long distance romance and parental disapproval, that is the easy part. I often thought it was appropriate that we met so close to the Mason-Dixon line. It seemed like the perfect place to start.

When I got married, my friends were quick to tease me about my loss of freedom, the ball and chain I would wear, and all of the other clichéd things guys feel obligated to say. Never once did I feel that way about marrying Jessica. As I approached middle age, I found many friends and acquaintances complaining—complaining about "the old lady," complaining about having to go to a "chick flick," complaining about their sex lives. These were the friends who didn't divorce.

I have no complaints. My life with Jessica, including our sex life, is still vibrant and vital and the most valued aspect of my existence. That's why I was so frightened when she withdrew, and why I worried so much about how she was handling her disappointment. It's what friends and lovers do, no matter which side of the Mason-Dixon line they grew up on.

CHAPTER 29

Dream Interrupted

Or: Reality Lights

This time it was Jodie Foster. She was singing to me, flirting with me, ready to take over where Julianne Moore had left off. This time it was the phone that ruined the moment. It was 5:30 a.m., half an hour before my alarm would ring. I was about to protest the loss of quality time with Jodie when I realized my wife was fully awake, more alert and intense than anyone should be at that hour. She gripped the receiver like it was a lifeline, as if letting go would cause her to drown, as if she were literally hanging on to every word coming through the receiver. By the time I noticed the keenness of her eyes and the firmness of her jaw, I was becoming alert and intense as well. When I gave her the questioning look, she mouthed the words, "Miss Leena."

I watched her listen; then heard her say, "Would you mind repeating that for my husband?" Apparently, Miss Leena did not mind, and the next thing I knew I was gripping the receiver while Miss Leena repeated the tale that would change our lives forever.

At approximately 10:45 p.m. last evening, the Shriners Hospital in Cincinnati received a phone call from a distraught woman named Arlene Crawford. She said her husband was headed for the hospital, that he was tired of his new daughter being four hours away, that he was bringing her home and that nobody was going to stop him. When she was asked if he had been drinking, she indicated that he had been, and that he had also taken, "Somethin', I can't say what, but I know it ain't good."

That phone call may have saved Donna Jo's life. If a chemically crazed man had charged into I.C.U. and started ripping out wires in an attempt to move a child who was not ready to be moved, who knows what might have happened, and who knows how traumatized she might have been.

Thanks to the phone call, security was ready. By the time Frank Crawford arrived, he had no chance of carrying out his plan, although he did not go quietly. Miss Leena had no idea what he had taken, since she was not there. Those who were could only speculate, but that speculation centered around P.C.P.—angel dust. Few other drugs would create the monster security encountered that evening. Mr. Crawford was strong beyond his size, and seemingly oblivious to the efforts of the officers. He kept yelling obscenities and twice threw a 250-pound guard to the ground. It took three officers and a stun gun to subdue him. Physically. They never did subdue his foul mouth as he screamed and spit and tried to bite those who finally succeeded in cuffing his hands and feet.

That was all Miss Leena knew. She said the nurses on duty had never seen a more violent encounter, and cringed at the thought of what might have been if Crawford had arrived without warning.

I thanked Miss Leena for the call, and we both promised to keep each other informed of any developments. I hung up the phone and turned slowly to face a trembling wife. "Adam … do you think … well … does this … I mean …"

"Yeah. Exactly." It was one of those non-sentence conversations that somehow precisely communicated what needed to be said. "Let's not get our hopes up too much, just in case." As soon as I said it I knew how dumb that sounded, since my heart was pounding to the rhythm of high hopes, and I knew hers was as well.

"We need to call Theresa."

"Agreed."

I got ready for work while Jessica woke up our lawyer. Theresa arranged a 10:00 meeting with Jessica and promised to begin work immediately. We decided that I would go to work, and Jessica would call me when she got through with Theresa.

Usually, I enjoy work. Usually, I am able to immerse myself in it, to lose track of time and place. Usually, I am able to focus. The day Miss Leena called was not a usual day, and I was never more unfocused. Anxiety kills concentration.

It was after noon when Jessica arrived at the store. I was helping a customer, so she motioned that she would meet me in the coffee shop. My desire to patiently help the slow, indecisive, talkative lady was non-existent, yet I remained surprisingly calm until she left.

Jessica was enjoying her vanilla latte when I joined her. "Have you eaten?"

"No, have you?"

"No, I just now came from Theresa's office."

"And?"

"And, let's go somewhere where you can't be interrupted."

"Give me ten minutes to make sure everything is covered." I could hardly stand the suspense, and I was back in four. I drove to a nearby deli, then a quiet park with a few picnic tables. Over pastrami and rye and soft drinks, Jessica detailed her eventful morning, becoming more animated as she continued.

By the time my wife had finished, I had as clear a picture as a non-participant could have. I also learned why the Crawfords were so interested in adopting a child they seemed so ill equipped to care for.

Donna Jo's father and mother had no property to speak of; only the lot was left. That lot had value, although not a lot, so to speak. It was enough money to interest Frank, and maybe Arlene, but Theresa always suspected there was something else. There was. It was a safety deposit box, a box that held an undisclosed amount of money, and some drugs. The idea of drugs being stashed in a bank deposit box shouldn't have seemed so weird, not that I know about those things, but it did.

The deposit box was the key, except there was no key, it must have perished in the fire, or else been so well hidden that nobody could find it. It took some time for Davis Richardson III to convince the bank that the Crawfords were the legal guardians of Donna Jo and the sole beneficiary of all the remaining assets, including the deposit box. Frank Crawford was finally given the key yesterday.

He celebrated by getting drunk. The staff at the hospital was right, he had used angel dust, for the first time ever according to Arlene. Theresa suspects that he beat his wife, but Arlene won't admit it. Once he got feeling like superman he drove to Cincinnati, actually drove for four hours without killing himself or anyone else.

It was Arlene's conscience, or perhaps her beating, that led to the phone call, which led to Frank's arrest. Theresa talked to Chief Mitchell, who said that Frank had to be restrained in his cell. He was as likely to hurt himself as he was others. He didn't calm down until early this morning, when he finally passed out. He was currently undergoing psychological testing.

The Department of Children's Services was contacted immediately. They currently have temporary, emergency custody. Chief Mitchell and Theresa told Jessica there is no way Donna Jo would ever be allowed to be with Frank and Arlene. We sat there trying not to get our hopes up, letting reality and likelihood wash over us. There was little need for conversation; closeness was the only requirement.

The rest of the week I somehow went to work, wandered through a few conversations with Theresa and Derek and Amy, and mostly waited and worried. We talked to Miss Leena daily. We wanted to visit, or at least talk to Donna Jo, but Theresa insisted we try to be patient. There still was a court order against our visitation.

It was Monday when we learned that another hearing had been set. It was Thursday when it took place. Theresa told us it would be brief, and she was correct. She did not tell us that Arlene Crawford and Davis Richardson III would be there. Ironically, it was their presence that made the hearing so brief.

Judge Clayborne gave a brief but accurate review of the last hearing and his decision. He detailed the, "New information that required a previous judgment be overturned." He further stated that he had signed statements by Mr. and Mrs. Crawford indicating their desire to relinquish any and all rights and claims and blah, blah, blah they are no longer in any custodial mumbo jumbo legalese, nor will they have visitation on and on, nor should they approach or talk to said minor child, detail, detail, finally done.

It was noted that Mr. Crawford, while still in custody, had voluntarily signed the statement, and Mrs. Crawford and her lawyer stated that yes, indeed, what the judge had read accurately reflected their intention, at which point new paper work was produced. The Department of Children's Services recommended that Adam and Jessica Donahue be awarded custody, and without objection, it was so ordered. The judge explained that it was a temporary order, that there would be periodic visits and reports by D.C.S., that after six months a permanent assignment could be made, and adoption proceedings could begin. He said other things about the previous decision and the mysterious way that justice works, but I was concentrating on my wife—my wife who had finally become a mom. I was a dad, and if I had cut the umbilical chord myself, I could not have been a prouder father.

As we were leaving the courtroom, Arlene Crawford walked by. She never made eye contact, never actually stopped walking, but she was able to mumble, "I'm sorry about all this. It was Frank's idea. You'll be better than we would have." With that she was gone, replaced by her lawyer.

Davis Richardson III did stop. He patted me on the back, did the same to my wife, as if we were old college pals, and had the nerve to gloat, "I'm glad for ya'll. I knew from the start you'd be good. I was just doing my job—nothing personal."

I started to respond, to tell that s.o.b. what I thought, but Jessica stopped me. "Don't you remember our arrangement?"

"Our arrangement?"

"Yes, our arrangement. The one we made in Cincinnati. You know, you'll do the heavy lifting, I'll take care of the light stuff."

The vague recollection of our first encounter with the Crawfords entered my mind, followed by a smile. "Yeah, I do."

"Well, honey, this is definitely light stuff." Then, with the sweetest smile, she oozed her Southern charm. "Why, Mr. Davis Richardson III, I declare. If you had your way, Donna Jo would have lived with a very dangerous man. Not personal? Of course it was personal. It could have been deadly." Then, as Richardson's smile faded and my wife turned to leave, she couldn't resist one final parting shot. "Oh, and my husband was right. You are a pompous ass."

I guess there is nothing like motherhood to make a woman frisky, at least motherhood that doesn't require a long labor. Although Jessica actually did go through a labor of sorts, it just wasn't physical. By the time we got to the car, we were giddy. We sped home, grabbed lunch and our suitcases and headed for a long weekend in Nashville. The phrase "pompous ass" seemed to emerge every fifty or sixty miles. There was no need for any form of bobble head ping-pong. Neither of us could concentrate. We were parents.

CHAPTER 30

Justice

Or: Justice

We were greeted by a jubilant Miss Leena. She hugged us so tight and congratulated us so sincerely that she reminded us of what it would be like to have a family. We had been so wrapped up in our own feelings we had forgotten the emotional toll all of this had taken on the only person who saw Donna Jo daily.

Miss Leena took us to see Donna Jo, who was asleep. We had been there before, but this time we were looking at our daughter. Miss Leena excused herself and left us to relish the moment. It wasn't long before Donna Jo awoke, clearly surprised to see us. She greeted us politely, but not warmly. She answered our questions about her health, but did not volunteer anything beyond what was called for. I suspect she felt betrayed by our long absence.

Fortunately, my wife knows children. In a language perfectly tailored for Donna Jo, she explained how sometimes adults have to do things they don't want to, how sometimes it takes a long time to do things that should not take so long, and how sometimes even adults make mistakes. She told her that she never wanted to stay away, that she couldn't help it. Then she said, "Today, something happened. Something wonderful." She explained what a judge does, and added, "The judge said you can live with us; that I can be with you always. Donna Jo, I promise, I will never leave you again."

"You promise?"

"Cross my heart."

"And I don't have to stay with Uncle Frank 'n Aunt Arlene?"

"No. Not now, not ever."

I hope the family that cries together stays together. I watched my daughter's face contort and tears stream down her cheeks, tears that released whatever pent up emotions a six-year-old burn victim with no family might harbor. Jessica was crying, and telling her it was okay, now, and I shed the first fatherly tears of my life, and Miss Leena came back and murmured, "Lord a mercy, if this ain't just about the most beautiful sight these tired ol' eyes have ever seen," and we all took turns huggin' and cryin' and letting the tears and the joy and the relief cleanse and calm our beings as they poured down like the first rain after a three month drought. It was the beginning, and in the beginning, it was good.

AFTER

CHAPTER 1

The Ordeal

Or: Rehab

I want progress to be linear. I have always wanted progress to be linear. I have always been disappointed.

Once we figured out certain prejudices were wrong, we should have marched in one straight line to total equality. It did not happen. There were starts and setbacks, like a child learning to walk. And Donna Jo's progress was every bit as non-linear as every other form of progress.

It began with the skin grafts. There was almost immediate progress from the day Mr. Henri Thakkurian said, "They've taken." Donna Jo was alert, happy, on the mend. Then there was infection, and fever, and setback. For one full week she lapsed in and out of consciousness as she was pumped full of life saving drugs. Drugs. She was in the hospital because of drugs. Her life now depended on drugs.

During the worst night, we watched helplessly as Donna Jo lie trembling, soaked in sweat. She began mumbling, incoherently at first, and then, clearly, hauntingly, "I'm sorry. I'll try harder, I'll be good, I'm sorry, I'll try harder, I'll be good." Over and over, like the mantra of a possessed spirit, "I'm sorry, I'll try harder, I'll be good."

And then she was quiet, and the sweating stopped, and she opened her eyes and we dared to breathe and hope again. It would be the last time she was unconscious, but not the last setback. It was a two-year ordeal, and only Jessica and Miss Leena saw every step of the earliest phase.

We were back to spending our weeks apart, me working, Jessica staying with our daughter. Our daughter. The first two or three hundred times I said those two words they sounded strangely comfortable, awkwardly natural, pleasantly unfamiliar. I spent much of that early period getting Donna Jo's bedroom ready for the day when she left the hospital. And once again, because they would not accept any other arrangement, I was back to Thursdays with Derek and Amy.

Donna Jo's skin was not her only problem. Physically, she was weak, the result of too much bed rest, too much weight loss, too much inactivity. No amount of muscle stimulation can take the place of being an active child. And her physical problems weren't confined to her external problems.

Donna Jo's lungs were an area of concern, and would remain so. Numerous respiratory specialists and therapists would become a part of her rehabilitation process. And her problems were not all physical.

No one knew exactly how much Donna Jo remembered about the fire, or her past. Her haunting, "I'm sorry, I'll try harder, I'll be good" was alarming. So were the facts of her young life. She lived with people who made and took and sold drugs. Even though their stupidity caused her to be seriously injured, they were her parents. She lost her home, her parents, and months of going to school, playing with friends, being a child. She hadn't skipped rope or played duck, duck, goose, or red rover, or tag. Her favorite teacher had stopped coming to see her. She had been told she was going to live with two people she didn't really care for. Then she was told that was all wrong, that her favorite teacher could see her, in fact, they would live together, but not right away. First, she had to undergo numerous operations. Some of her good skin was removed and placed where her burns were. She hurt, and she was beginning to worry about one of the worst things a girl could ever have to worry about, even at six. She worried that she might be ugly. She might be different, bad, an outcast. She didn't know the word hideous, but she worried about it anyway. So the mental scarring needed treatment, also.

Still, it was rehabilitation; rehab. And rehab, though arduous and exhausting, is superior to being unable to rehab. Being able to rehab also meant no need to be in I.C.U. Not needing I.C.U. meant not being cared for by Miss Leena. I was not there for the tearful good-bye. Even Donna Jo, who had been comatose much of the time, seemed to sense the significance this loyal, dedicated, loving professional had played in her life. Miss Leena handled the situation with her usual style. "Now you know you're only three floors above me.

I'll see you every day, I promise. So there is not need to go boo-hooin' and all." Of course, that didn't stop her from wiping her eyes.

People make promises. People break promises. We learn early, often from our parents. "I'll do it later, I'll come to your game, you can do that when you're older." Guys learn quickly, especially when females are involved. "I'll call you, you're special, I'll respect you in the morning." Businesses make promises to customers, promises they can't keep. Workers promise deliveries, or appointment times, and don't come through. Political promises have the half-life of a snowball in July.

Miss Leena made promises. Miss Leena kept promises, and not once was I surprised. Only grateful. Grateful to have her in my life. In all of our lives. Grateful for the many like her who touched lives. I can't even mention nurses' salaries without wanting to scream.

We lived for milestones—the first or the last of anything related to Donna Jo's progress; the last day of an I.V., the first day she walked without help. Jessica said it was like really watching a child take her first steps.

Donna Jo could not have been a better patient when her therapy started. She worked with a passion, a passion made of a promise that her work would lead to her release from the hospital. Jessica was able to notice the daily progress. For me, each weekend marked monumental improvement. It was strange to see her upright, walking, gaining weight, and smiling, always smiling. Color had returned to her face, sparkle had returned to her eyes, and enthusiasm had returned to her spirit. Miss Leena returned to her room everyday, and I returned every weekend, to watch a fragile but determined six-year-old fight to regain and reclaim some semblance of normalcy.

Donna Jo's facial scar was significant. It started under her left ear, spread to the corner of her mouth, and headed south to the tip of her chin. Most of the left side of her neck was also scarred. Fortunately, she did not seem to have serious pain from this area. The only other lasting scarring involved her left arm, stretching inches above and below her elbow. This area did give her pain, and she often carried her arm close to her body in a protective manner.

Psychologically, she seemed to epitomize the resiliency of youth. She had moments, at night, in the dark, when she feared some unseen and unknown force, but that was to be expected.

Then, one bright Thursday morning in May, she was discharged. She would continue therapy, but at home, in Knoxville. In fact, she would be home before Mother's Day.

CHAPTER 2

Atticus

Or: Bobbling On

Donna Jo was like John Denver when he discovered the Rocky Mountains, "Coming home to a place she'd never been before." She was genuinely pleased with her room, her new house, her yard. But most of all, she looked forward to meeting the dog she had heard so much about.

Atticus is a typical Golden Retriever. He bounds out of his kennel, ready to share his enthusiasm with the person who freed him. Sometimes that bounding enthusiasm takes on the subtlety of a blitzing linebacker. I was a little concerned about him blitzing Donna Jo, who would be the first child he had been with. There really was no reason to be concerned.

Sometimes, people drive me crazy when they talk about their pets. They attribute such deep motives and thought processes to their animals that it becomes comical. And if there are several of them, they all try to top each other. I've often been tempted to say, "My dog used the quadratic formula," or, "My dog knows where Jimmy Hoffa is buried. He tries to tell me, but I don't speak canine," or "My dog lies awake at night, staring at the stars while contemplating the origin of the universe," but of course, I never do. Mostly because I know the pet owners wouldn't think it was funny, or else they'd find some way to top it.

I mention all of that as a prelude to what happened when Atticus met Donna Jo. He did indeed come bounding out of his kennel, thanking Jessica and I in his usual manner. Then he bounded toward Donna Jo, who was not only taken aback but actually stepped back, not sure what to make of him, only to have him slow down, calmly walk to her, smelling her, tail wagging steadily.

"He's big."

"Yes, he is."

"Will he bite me?"

"No. He's very friendly, and he doesn't bite. Besides, he likes you."

"How do you know?"

"Because his tail is wagging, and he's waiting for you to pet him. Go ahead."

With that, Donna Jo timidly put her right hand on his head, her left arm remaining at her side. Atticus kept inching closer, until he was close enough to give her the first "dog kiss" she ever received. In that instant, some cosmic form of bonding took place, as if Atticus sensed a need to be calm and gentle with this small person standing by him.

I sometimes think that our dog was the best part of our daughter's therapy. They truly romped together, exploring the backyard and the woods. I sensed a joy and a relief in Donna Jo whenever she and Atticus were together.

We had talked with Donna Jo about adoption. She seemed to like the idea, including the part about changing her last name, but I'm not sure she fully understood it. It seemed to come in waves of understanding, like its reality or finality was seeping in to her awareness. One night, when Jessica was reading to her, she asked, "What will I call you? I mean after I'm adopted?"

"What would you like to call me?"

"Well, I'd like to call you ..." She stopped. Clearly she was uncomfortable with what she wanted to say.

"Go on."

"Would it be okay if I called you mom?"

"It would be wonderful if you called me that."

"When will I be adopted?"

"It could be a few more months."

"Oh."

"Donna Jo?"

"Yes?"

"You don't have to wait. You can call me that now if you want to."

"I can?"

"Yes."

"Honest?"

"Honest."

And with that, Donna Jo began to cry. She had felt motherless for too long. She felt that she might remain motherless.

I must admit, I felt a tinge of jealousy for a while, but several days later, as she sat on my lap, she began the exploration again, only I was to have a different outcome.

"What should I call you?"

"What would you like to call me?"

She looked into my eyes, placing her forehead against mine, touching my face before pulling back and saying, "How about Mr. Bobble Head?"

"Mr. Bobble Head?"

"Yeah, Mr. Bobble Head." With that, she gently pushed the top of my head, and I began to do my best bobble. This was not the first time. In fact, it had become somewhat of a routine, one I had started in the hospital. Still, it continued to get a laugh, along with her usual, "You're so silly." It wasn't what I had expected, but if it made her laugh, I was for it. She ran to tell Jessica, then returned to jump on my lap, waiting for her mom to follow so we could demonstrate.

For two weeks I was Mr. Bobble Head. Then, one evening on our front porch, with Atticus lying between us, his head resting on Donna Jo's lap, she said, "Mr. Bobble Head is okay for make-believe, but I want a not make-believe name to call you."

"I see. Do you have anything in mind?"

"Well, if I'm calling Mrs. Donahue, mom ..."

"Yes?"

"And you are married ..."

"Uh ha"

"Well, would it be okay if I called you dad?"

"It would make me very happy if you called me dad."

She didn't cry this time, but she looked up at me with those melt-your-heart eyes, and I found a way to reach over Atticus and hug her, and kiss her forehead, only to have the dog sit up so that he could receive some affection also.

The Department of Children's Services conducted several visitations. In July, we went to yet another hearing, where reports were read and papers were signed and our daughter legally became Donna Jo Donahue. It was nice to have it finalized, but I didn't need a court to tell me what I already knew. I was a dad. I was a dad because my heart said so. I was a dad because every joy my little girl experienced became my joy, every pain she felt became my pain. I was a dad because Donna Jo had declared it so, on our front porch, while petting our dog. She had far more authority than any judge.

CHAPTER 3

Catch Up

Or: Bloody Wigglin'

The therapy continued, but now with an additional component. My wife had completed all of the necessary paperwork to receive permission to home school our daughter. Neither of us wanted this. Both of us looked forward to the day when Donna Jo would go to the public school, and be with other students, and be just like any other kid. But she wasn't ready for that yet.

Our daughter was behind. She needed to continue catching up physically. She also needed the individual attention that a trained educator could give her. Donna Jo accepted this like she accepted every other aspect of her new life, with optimism and enthusiasm. How is it that kids who have no idea what the words optimism and enthusiasm mean can so typify or exemplify those characteristics?

Jessica was a taskmaster, but she had a willing student. Donna Jo needed the individual attention. Jessica needed to teach. Together, they thrived.

They reviewed the kindergarten readiness activities, then began the all-important first grade curriculum. Before long, Donna Jo was reading. She was printing. She was learning about numbers, about plants and animals and people in her community. They took field trips together, to Ijams Nature Center and the Knoxville Zoo. And they painted. Donna Jo quickly discovered that she and her mother shared a love for art, and many evenings I would return from work to find one or both of them at the easel. That was the beauty of their arrangement. Teaching and learning had no time limits, no boundaries, and no distractions. It also provided an opportunity to grow closer. Theirs was the best student-teacher relationship. I tried not to be jealous.

I also tried not to play the "what if" game, but I failed. I found myself asking, "What if there had been no fire? What if Donna Jo had simply grown up in a meth-controlled environment? What if there had been a fire and she ended up with the Crawfords? What if she had never entered our lives?"

The music began by accident. Jessica and I were cleaning out the garage. Our "helpers," Donna Jo and Atticus, were supervising, when an old keyboard caught our daughter's eye. "What's that?"

"That old thing? It's a keyboard."

"What's a keyboard?"

"It's like a small piano. Your mom use to play, back when she thought she was going to be a rock and roll star."

"What's that mean?"

"It means your mom use to play music. Loud music."

"Can I hear some?"

The keyboard still worked, although the sound wasn't much. A good cleaning and some minor repairs produced a passable tone, and Donna Jo was hooked. Music became part of her daily routine, and then part of her passion. She would stare at Jessica's hands, mesmerized by their movement and their ability to produce sound. It was a logical progression for her to try, and before long, "Twinkle, Twinkle Little Star" and "Mary Had a Little Lamb" were being hammered out. Finding that keyboard for Donna Jo was like waking up to a room full of rainbows and shooting stars and four leaf clovers. It was lucky, and it was unforgettable.

So the lessons continued. More reading, more math, more elementary science and social studies. More trips, to libraries and museums and planetariums. More painting. More music. More growth. I did not realize how much a child is able to learn at that age. I always knew that my wife had special talents as an educator, but it is different when one gets to observe it for oneself. I found myself cherishing every moment, every change, every step of the developmental journey I had always taken for granted. I found myself feeling cheated. I, we, had missed those first six steps, those so-called "formative years." How many milestones, how much growth, how much wonder and amazement did we not get to experience?

Miss Leena called weekly. Sometimes, Donna Jo would read to her, or bang out something on the keyboard for her, or tell her about her latest painting, or her latest adventure with Atticus. Jessica always thanked her for calling. Miss

Leena always thanked Jessica for allowing her to continue to share in the journey. It was, she claimed, the reason she was a nurse.

It was not all positive. As Donna Jo grew, as she got closer to the day she would return to the public school, our greatest fear became reality. We worried about how people would react to her physical appearance. We still noticed the scars, they had not faded much, but they were not a focal point. They were a small part of the whole. But strangers were different, and cruel. In the heart of the Bible belt, my daughter was a curiosity at best, a monster at worse.

In my wife's kindergarten class, before the fire, Donna Jo had been an outgoing, social, friendly child. She had been well liked by the other children. We knew she was ready to be that person again. We feared what might happen.

Our first preview of coming attractions came at a shoe store. It was Saturday morning, and I had taken Donna Jo to, well to buy shoes, because that's what they have at shoe stores. I didn't really notice at first, I was too busy being all cool and parental on my first major outing, feeling great about this unique bonding experience and all that other clichéd stuff. I was observant enough to notice Donna Jo literally moving closer to me, spending less time looking at shoes, more time looking at me. That's when I noticed the problem. Other kids. There was a woman in the store, and she had two children with her. The woman quickly looked away when I made eye contact with her, but the kids continued to stare. It made me uncomfortable, so I imagined how my daughter felt.

I was able to distract her, and we went about the process of selecting her very own sneakers that had the perfect color and size and feel and style and whatever else is involved with finding the perfect shoe that will be worn out or outgrown in no time. I'd forgotten the staring trio until we went to pay for our purchase. The woman and her two children were in front of us. The woman was paying, but the two children were staring. Again.

Donna Jo saw it, and moved behind me. I stared back. My eyes grew wide. I began to flare my nostrils, in and out. Next, I began to employ a talent I hadn't used since junior high school. I began to wiggle my ears. I had the whole thing going, eyes poppin; (although not literally), nostrils flarin', ears wigglin'. That's when Momma Bear turned around. I thought laughter was the perfect solution, but Momma Bear apparently disagreed. She huffed (but didn't puff or blow the store down), and pushed her cubs toward the door, the word "weirdo" cascading from her lips. I was about to laugh and high-five Donna Jo, but was stopped by the, "Did you see her face" and the word "gross" as the door closed behind them.

The man at the counter saw the entire thing, but said nothing. He made no eye contact as he rang up the price and took our money.

It was a terrible ride home. It began in silence. Silence gave way to tears, and tears to the simple but poignant, "They stared at me. They think I'm ugly."

I said all of the things you say when you can't find the right words. I used all of the words about her beauty in my eyes, all of the comments about rude people and kind people, and everything I knew that said, "I love you."

It didn't help. By the time we got home, a sad little girl went to her room, dropped the shoebox on her floor, and went outside to play with Atticus, still wearing her old shoes. I told Jessica about it. She knew this kind of thing was coming, but I still ached for her. My hurt had turned to anger, and I let loose. "You should have seen them. So cruel. So heartless. I could almost accept it from the kids, but the mother was no better."

"Sometimes people don't realize what they're doing."

"Sometimes people are assholes."

"Don't you mean a cow's ass?"

"Not in this case. And I'll bet you tomorrow morning her kids are in Sunday school and she's in the amen corner, singin' about love and kindness and everything."

"You may be right. But Adam?"

"Yeah?"

"It's going to happen again, and maybe we need to talk about how to handle it. I mean, not everyone can wiggle their bloody ears."

I love my wife. She is smart and funny and knows how to calm me down when I get too bloody dramatic.

That night, she began a discussion about what had happened. She talked about rude people, about how we all have things that make us different, how sometimes we have to accept things we don't like. She talked about other people who may be blind, or deaf, or in a wheelchair, and how some people, some cruel people, make fun of them, also. Or they might make fun of people because they have a different color, or a different accent, or different clothes. She said the important thing was to know that she was loved; that her mother and father knew she had scars when they chose her, and they did choose her.

She seemed happier when she went to bed. She even called me an ear wiggling bobble head, which I thought was accurate. It was still another two days before she wore her new shoes. It will take years before I forget about ol' Momma Bear.

There are some people who know, just instinctively know what to say, when to say it, and how to say it. Sometimes, they might say the same thing someone else would say, only it sounds better coming from them. My wife is one of those people, and Donna Jo and I are better for it. Even her skills would be tested.

CHAPTER 4

The Party

Or: Breakfast at Donna Jo's

The party was Jessica's idea. It was one of those serene Southern nights, just perfect for porch sitting. I had long since discovered that I had a particular talent for this activity, and I tried to maximize my skill.

Donna Jo was in bed. Atticus was asleep next to my front porch rocking chair. Jessica was sitting in her hanging hammock seat. There was a slight breeze. It was that perfectly lazy time, warm but not too humid, when the cicadas were just warming up, and the occasional call of the screech owl and the unmatched beauty of the stars weaved their spells. We rocked quietly, absorbed in our personal reveries, until Jessica, almost apologetically, broke the spell.

"I think I have an idea about how to smooth Donna Jo's transition to school."

Donna Jo's "transition" was the primary topic in our house. The incident in the shoe store had been a test, one I had failed. "I was about to say, 'I'm all ears,' but somehow I think I'd rather just let you tell me your plan."

Jessica complimented my judgment before detailing her idea. My wife had been in close contact with the school. Her goal was for Donna Jo to enter third grade. In other words, her energies would enable our daughter to rejoin the class with which she had started school. This would be an amazing accomplishment. Donna Jo would have to pass the tests given at school, but there was no doubt she would be ready for third grade.

Jessica would talk to the principal and the third grade teacher. She felt that there would be some students who had been in kindergarten with Donna Jo. It was her hope that she could select three or four classmates, discuss the situation with their parents, and invite them to a back to school party at our house.

I thought it was a brilliant plan, and told her so. She wasn't finished. She wanted Derek and Amy to come over after the kids' party, just in case things didn't go well. And she had one more idea. "I would love to have Miss Leena visit. If we pick the right day, I'll bet she'll come. What do you think?"

"I think I want you. I may make love to you right here—in my rockin' chair."

"I'll take that as an endorsement of my plan."

We didn't use the rocking chair, but after waking up Atticus so he could walk to his kennel and go back to sleep, we did find a more conventional area to finish the endorsement, which was wise, middle-age flexibility being what it is.

Donna Jo amazed the test-givers, and she was officially enrolled in third grade. She met her teacher, Mrs. Larsen, a dynamo who could not have been friendlier. Everyone liked the idea of the party, and Mrs. Larsen not only helped select four students, she promised to bake cookies and attend the gathering.

Having Donna Jo in our lives became a new routine, something so wonderfully familiar we wondered how we ever lived without her. The first time she met Derek and Amy, it was like a reunion with people she'd never met before. They acted like long-lost relatives, or maybe short-lost relatives. Derek teased her and joked with her, and beginning with the second meeting, always seemed to have some small item to give her. I once joked, "I wonder what ol' Uncle Derek has this time."

Donna Jo's eyes widened. "Is he really my uncle?"

I started to explain that he really wasn't, that it was just a figure of speech, but Derek interrupted. "I'll be her uncle if she wants me to. Shoot fire, why not?"

That's all it took. Derek became Uncle Derek, and when his wife demanded equal time, so she became Aunt Amy, pronounced like the bug, ant, not like the Massachusetts aunt, which rhymes with font. I can still hear my mother saying, "Aunts are people, ants are bugs." She would have hated Andy Griffith and Ant Bea. I love using the Southern pronunciation, especially since it would have bugged my mother, so to speak.

Miss Leena was thrilled with the invitation. She promised to attend, and asked if she could bring a guest, peaking our curiosity. That's when Jessica decided that Theresa had to attend, also. Theresa said she would, only she'd be late.

So it came to pass, two weeks before the first day of school, that the Donahue family hosted four other third grade girls. The parents all knew Jessica from kindergarten. They were curious to see Donna Jo, and usually lingered enough to check her out. Then they'd leave, promising to return at 5:00, the official end of the party.

Each classmate-to-be reacted the same. She would study Donna Jo's face and ask a question like, "Does it hurt?" or "Does it feel weird?" or "Can I touch it?" Donna Jo would answer, the girl would reply, "Oh," or, "Cool" and then they would run off. The girls did not walk anywhere. They ran to Donna Jo's bedroom; then outside to meet Atticus, then back to the bedroom for some forgotten item, then back outside. I was beginning to question our sanity when Mrs. Larsen arrived. We served pizza, she told stories and answered all of their questions about third grade, then they sang songs and ate the cookies she had baked, and before we knew it, Donna Jo looked like any other kid playing with her friends. It brought back the memory of that most primitive yet powerful desire to be accepted, to simply fit in. I'm not sure I remembered, or even knew how silly third graders can be, but suddenly there were giggles, and whispered secrets, and more giggles, and a language that sounded something like English, but I couldn't understand it. Then they started running around again, chasing Atticus and trying to dress him up in Donna Jo's clothes, and then a parent came, and then another, until glorious calm returned, and Atticus had the chance to lie down and go to sleep.

Mrs. Larsen declared the party a success. We were all pleased with the interaction, and grateful for her participation. Shortly after she left, Uncle Derek and Aunt Amy arrived. This time he had brought her a diary, something that big girls write in. She hugged him, climbing up in his lap to tell him all about her party and her friends and how she would write all about it in her present. Then she climbed onto Amy's lap and they talked about each girl, each name, each personality, and clothing, and hair, and they might still be talking if the doorbell hadn't rung.

We had told Donna Jo that Derek and Amy were coming. She did not know about Miss Leena. When Jessica wondered who that could be, and asked Donna Jo to help her find out, she didn't know what to expect. When Donna Jo saw Miss Leena, she screamed her name and literally jumped for joy. She was so excited she barely noticed the bald, handsome, barrel-chested black man who was with her. I walked to him, introduced myself and held out my hand, saying, "Let me guess. Police Chief LaMarcus J. Mitchell. Am I right?"

"No, sir. I never heard that name. Leena, you been seein' someone else?"

Just as that both feet in the mouth feeling started to settle into my stomach, Miss Leena slapped his broad shoulder. "LaMarcus, you behave, you hear? How ya gonna tease a man you don't know? First words, the very first words he hear outa your mouth is foolishness."

I liked him immediately. Miss Leena was carrying on about how much Donna Jo had grown, and how pretty she was, so I steered the chief into the room and introduced him to the Pearsons. Miss Leena was abducted, led away by the arm to visit Donna Jo's room. The chief wanted to know how I knew his identity.

"It was deductive reasoning, quite elementary actually." It is amazing how quickly friends will turn on you, so eventually I confessed to guessing, although I had remembered Theresa talking about the chief, and how differently Officer Mitchell had treated her once he had Miss Leena's statement.

Since we weren't big talkers, not in a boastful sense, and since anyone can engage in small talk, we sat around making medium talk. We told the chief, who insisted we call him LaMarcus, how much we loved Miss Leena. He insisted we call her Leena. I could have told him that I had no problem calling him my his first name, and would do so, but that calling his date anything but *Miss Leena* would seem wrong, maybe even blasphemous. Of course, I didn't actually tell him that. I just could have, if I needed to. I think that says something about who has real power and authority, but I'm not sure exactly what.

Donna Jo finally allowed Miss Leena to return. She stayed with us for a while before excusing herself. She wanted to watch T.V. and write in her diary, which she did until Theresa arrived.

My daughter knew that Theresa was a lawyer, even if she wasn't sure what that meant. She knew that Theresa had something to do with her living with us, even if she had no idea what. All she really knew was that we liked her, and that was good enough for her. Again she socialized with us before excusing herself one more time.

The adult party featured hors d'oeuvres and pizza and barbequed ribs and beer and wine and dessert. Donna Jo fell asleep watching T.V., woke up long enough to kiss every person goodnight, and then climbed on my shoulders for a ride to bed. "Daddy today was fun. I like having people come to our house."

"I like it, too."

"Yeah. It's special."

I think she was still awake when I kissed her goodnight. I don't think she was awake when I closed her door. I returned to hear Theresa say, "She is so wonderful. You are so lucky; and so is she."

Jessica answered for both of us, "We know how lucky we are. And it's not just because of Donna Jo. It's also because of friends like you."

That was the extent of the sentimentality, no matter how truthful it was. Derek and LeMarcus took turns trying to outdo each other with funny stories, occasionally letting Amy and Miss Leena interject some nursing humor. We stayed up past midnight, and everyone stayed at our house rather than risk driving home. Donna Jo could not believe everyone was still there when she awoke the next morning. Early. And once Donna Jo was awake, it wasn't long before everyone was awake.

We had a wonderful breakfast before everyone went back to their own houses and their own world of work and problems and occasional insanity, except for LaMarcus, who saw insanity far more frequently than the rest of us.

It had been one of those rare events, where the outcome exceeded the expectation, where the actual participation was superior to the plan. I try to remind myself of those days when the equal and opposite reaction occurs. I don't always remember.

CHAPTER 5

School

Or: Numb Nuts

Going back to school had new meaning at our house. For most kids, it means a return to the next grade after summer vacation. For Donna Jo, it meant a return after a two-year absence. She had survived her burns, and physical therapy, and home schooling. Could she survive third grade? Would there be more days like her party, or more days like the shoe store? Academically, she was fine. Would she remain so? How would she do socially?

Jessica and I never got to experience the first day of nursery school, or the first day of kindergarten with our child, but I doubt that it would have been any different than the first time we watched Donna Jo wave good-bye as she walked onto that big yellow bus that met a small group of children a few hundred yards from our house.

I hate overly protective parents, yet I felt like a walking contradiction that day, every protective instinct in my body on full alert, working overtime. I also felt a sense of pride, even triumph. Thanks to my wife, and Miss Leena, and Dr. Thakkurian, and Theresa, Donna Jo was making her triumphant return to Cedar Valley Elementary School, and I wanted trumpets to be blaring and rose petals strewn in her path. A proclamation or two was in order, and a small parade wasn't out of the question. I settled for the proverbial and clichéd lump in my throat. Not all clichés are bad.

I was about to congratulate my wife, and tell her how proud I was of her and our daughter when another parent approached us. She had been standing near the bus stop, on the opposite side of the road. She walked up to us and, without a hello or an introduction or any customary social grace asked, "Is your kid the one with the, ah, um …"

"Scars?" I thought I'd help her out, since it was obvious what she meant. The pointing to the facial area gave it away.

"Yeah, scars. Is she your'n?"

"She is our daughter."

"Listen, I don't mean nothin'. I'm just askin', ya know? Is she, uh, you know, is she okay?"

"She's fine. They don't hurt. But thanks for asking." Somehow, I knew that wasn't what she meant, which is why I said it.

"That's not what I'm askin'. What I'm wantin' to know is she okay, you know." With that she began tapping the side of her head.

"You mean her hair? It's real." I was fighting the rising anger, but hoping not to show it. It was clear where this conversation was going.

It was equally clear that our neighbor did not appreciate my attempt at humor. "I don't care nothin' bout her dad gum hair. I want to know if she's dangerous, or crazy. Is she normal?"

"Are you?"

"What?"

"Are you? Normal?"

"I don't think I like your sassy attitude. You sound like a Yankee."

It was Jessica's turn. "Honey, I ain't no Yankee. Now, what the man was askin' was do you consider yourself normal? 'Cause if you is, she ain't."

"What's that suppose to mean?"

"It means that my daughter has skin damage from a fire. It means that normal people don't think someone is mentally ill, or dangerous, because of a few scars. It means that she is as normal as any child at this bus stop, and any of the parents."

"Well you don't need to get all huffy 'bout it. I was just askin'."

"No. You were just accusin' without knowin'. But we appreciate your concern and your compassion. You have a good day."

With that, we were gone, leaving ol' numb nuts for the greener pastures of our house. I love the phrase numb nuts, especially for people like her. We fumed awhile, and since I had arranged to be late for work anyway, I lingered long enough to therapy bitch. Therapy bitching is the cleansing ritual that changes nothing but feels wonderful. By the time I was done, I was able to put things in better perspective. I was not about to let one ignorant woman ruin our landmark day.

Numb Nuts stuck. I mean as a name, or nickname, or an identity. Long after we learned our neighbor's name (Debbie James) and her son's name (Kenny, although we preferred Jesse) we still called her Numb Nuts—or N.N. for short. It didn't take long to discover that Kenny was no prize. He was loud, pushy, and rude, especially to Donna Jo. Not that it was a surprise. We referred to him as junior, as in Numb Nuts, Jr. It was like watching a feeder system, or a training program, or a junior varsity insensitivity team.

We had wanted Donna Jo to ride the bus for the social aspect, and to have her have as "normal" an experience as possible. We learned that "normal" was a myth, especially at the bus stop. Since every other aspect of third grade was successful, we decided our daughter did not need to ride the bus. Jessica would drive her both ways, and the wheels on the bus could go round and round without her.

Mrs. Larsen was everything we could have hoped for. Donna Jo thrived. She went to her first sleepover in September, returned the favor in October, and played the part of the best-darned Pilgrim that ever was in her class' Thanksgiving play.

It was Norman Rockwellian, with a few smudges in the painting. Early one morning we awoke to some noise, and the sound of Atticus barking. Night animals would, occasionally, set him off, so we didn't think much of it, especially since doing something would mean leaving the warmth of our bed. It wasn't until I left for work that I discovered the cause of the commotion. Our mailbox had been destroyed, beaten, smashed, annihilated. I wondered if it was self-defense. I wasn't pleased, especially since ours was the only victim. Not that I wanted others to be violated. It just seemed like we were singled out, and that felt weird.

I would have bet money on one of the Numb Nuts Clan, and I was even more convinced when ol' Junior rode by while I was putting up the new box. "Somebody smash your mailbox?"

"Yeah, you have any idea who?"

"Nope. Could a been just about anybody, I guess."

I didn't want to pursue it any farther with our pal, especially since he had a certain smirk, like he was gloating over something. He stood with a leg on each side of his bike, than shifted his weight to one side as he prepared to mount his steed and ride off into his own mindset. I guess he felt obligated to offer a parting shot. "Maybe somebody don't like scar-faced Yankees." With those words he was gone, pedaling hard and laughing harder.

In my head I knew it didn't prove he had done anything. In my head, Jessica's long-standing advice about avoiding a pissing match with a skunk echoed there. In my head, I considered the source. But in my heart, I wanted to slap his chunky little Numb Nut face, at least momentarily. I finished installing the new mailbox and hurried to see my wife. I needed some maturity therapy.

The mailbox incident hurt. Not because of some sentimental attachment to the old box, or the cost of the new one. It was the violence of it, the personal nature of it, and the "scar-faced Yankee" insult of it.

Eventually I chalked it up as one of those random acts of stupidity that serves as the root canal of daily living. Then I came out of work and found my truck had a flat tire.

I parked on the side of our store, as do all of the employees, as a courtesy to our customers. The truck is hidden from view. I hurriedly removed the flat tire and put on one of the dumbest inventions in history—the donut spare. I drove to a tire center, where I was informed, "This tire was slashed. Look." In my haste I had missed the obvious. Clearly, this was not a case of running over a nail. Someone had actually slashed my tire.

I arrived home with a new tire and an old problem. I felt like I was being picked on. One thing was clear. Junior didn't drive to my work to flatten my tire, and I doubted if his mother did either. I could not find a link between my mailbox and my tire. I should have. It was a mistake that would prove fatal.

CHAPTER 6

Willie Mays

Or: Take Two and Hit to Right

The greatest baseball player I ever saw was Willie Mays. Not many kids in Massachusetts worshipped him like I did, not when he was playing three thousand miles away. But Willie was my first childhood hero. Nobody could hit and run and field like Willie.

I met him once. It was in a mall, where he was signing autographs for money that went to some charity. He was much older and heavier than the hero of my youth, but he still had that "Say-Hey" smile, and it was an emotional moment as I looked into the eyes of a legend and shook the once powerful hand of a true Giant. I framed his autographed photo, and found the perfect spot for it on my mantel, or Mantle, as the case may be. I kept my only possession from high school next to the fireplace. It's a thirty-three inch, thirty-two ounce baseball bat—Willie Mays model. I have no yearbooks, no high school ring, no letter sweaters. Just Willie.

Through little league playing and high school bench-sitting and little league coaching, Willie was "the man." I thought of him every time I sat in my chair and saw his picture or my old bat. I never thought Willie Mays would save my life.

The older I get, the stranger I sleep. Gone are the days of sleeping through a fire alarm (a college accomplishment) or any number of house jarring thunderstorms. I still fall asleep easily, but sometimes I wake up in the middle of the night and have trouble getting back to sleep. That's when I usually think about the Great American Novel (hereafter, the G.A.N.). Not that I actually put any words on paper. I usually just write in my mind.

It was December first. At 1:00 a.m. I used the bathroom. I don't know how long it took me to get back to sleep. At 2:30 I was awake again. That's when I heard something in the backyard, something that sounded like metal scraping. A moment later I heard a voice.

Jessica did not have trouble sleeping. I slipped from our bed, threw on some clothes, and stealthily headed toward the door. At the last second, I grabbed Willie Mays.

I went out the front door, greeted by a brisk breeze on a star-lit night. I stood listening. I had just about convinced myself that I had been imagining things when I heard footsteps, quickly coming along the side of the house. Willie Mays and I eased off the front porch and headed to the corner of the house. Next thing I knew, I was face-to-face with Frank Crawford.

I cannot describe the chilling affect his presence had on me. How was he not in jail? What was he doing in my backyard? And then, with horror, why hadn't Atticus barked? I guess I said his name out loud as I started to move past our intruder. That's when I noticed the knife, and heard a slurred, "You ain't goin nowhere. I'm fixin' to spill your guts right here. Ain't no women here to protect you this time." He was smiling, almost laughing as he slowly waved the knife back and forth, almost hypnotically. Then he lunged at me.

I was aware of a burning sensation on my forearm, and a sticky substance that followed immediately. I don't think I ever consciously registered the fact that my forearm had been cut, but on some instinctive level I'm sure I knew. I suspect that sense triggered the adrenalin rush that followed. Crawford was animated, alarmingly so, and he rushed toward me, slashing and slicing the air as he moved in for the kill. This time I was ready, and as he lunged toward me I quickly sidestepped his approach. That's when Willie Mays took over.

His momentum sent him past me, and Willie connected across the back of his shoulders. He staggered, fell to one knee, pivoted and jumped to his feet, glaring and snarling and repeating his slashing and slicing movements as he moved toward me once again. He was panting, gasping, "You … son … of … a …"

He never finished his thought. I used Willie more like a cue stick than a baseball bat, putting the barrel into his forehead with enough force to stagger him. Then I swung again. He reflex action caused his left hand, the one holding the knife, to rise toward his head. I connected with his arm, causing the knife to go flying from his hand as he howled in pain. That's when I kicked. I kicked him with a speed and a force and an accuracy that a martial arts student would have envied. I kicked him where the Frank Crawfords of the world deserve to be kicked, in his most private and painful part.

Crawford dropped to both knees, and for a moment, I was back in tee-ball, and his head was at the perfect height. It was at that exact moment when my front door opened and Jessica looked out. I do not know what would have happened if she hadn't opened the door. I'd like to think I would not have taken the swing, the swing that might have killed a man. I'd like to think that I was still somewhat in control of my emotions. In the slow motion replay, I see him drop to his knees. I feel more hatred and anger than I have ever felt. I feel my grip tighten on the handle; I feel the bat go back, cocked, ready to spring forward. I think I even start the motion, but I hear the door open, I check my swing, I yell, "Call 911 and then go get Atticus," and I see the terror in Frank Crawford's eyes, and I yell, "Lie down," and I see him start to but I kick him in the back, between his shoulders, because he's not moving quick enough, and I stand over him as he lies face down on my front lawn and I tell him if he so much as moves I'll knock his fucking head off, and I tap the back of it with the bat for emphasis, and I know I really could do it, and I know that he knows it, too. I wonder what would have happened if Jessica had not come to the door, and I'd like to think I wouldn't have swung, but I don't think that's the truth, and I wonder what it would be like to live with the knowledge that I killed a man, even a scum bag like Frank Crawford, and I'm glad I'll never know, and I wonder when the police will get here, and I wonder if Atticus is okay, and I realize I am bleeding and getting dizzy, and I never let my eyes leave the back of Crawford's head, and just as the knowledge that I might pass and give him the chance to finish the job registers, the police arrive. They cuff Crawford, who seems to have a broken arm, and they find his knife, and I think one of them tries to help me, but I'm running to the backyard, and I see Jessica in tears, and Atticus is trying to stand, and he appears drunk, and just as I get close to him, I stagger, and everything goes black.

CHAPTER 7

Aftermath

Or: Mockingbirds and Other Sins

I awoke in the emergency room, an I.V. in my right arm, a heavy wrap on my left. Jessica was seated next to me, smiling at my consciousness. "You're going to be fine, but you had a nasty cut. Very deep."

"Atticus?"

Her face told me more than her words. "He's at the all night hospital. He drank a lot of antifreeze. They're trying, but …"

"Where's Donna Jo?"

"At our house, with Amy. She never woke up."

"What time is it?"

"It's about 6:30."

"So what happens when she does wake up?"

"I don't know. Amy will figure it out."

Donna Jo was always awake by seven. She awoke happy, as if to say, "I'm ready world, show me what you've got." I have never met a person who awoke more genuinely pleasant. I was envious of her ability to begin the day that way. Most of us need caffeine and several hours to catch up to her. The thought of her waking up without us bothered me. The thought of her finding out about Atticus broke my heart. "Fill me in on what I missed."

Jessica sighed, an understandable preparation for reliving something she'd rather not. "The first thing I heard were footsteps—someone or something moving outside. You weren't in bed, and I was up when I heard a man yell. I opened the door and saw you about to decapitate Frank Crawford. Then you yelled for me to call the cops, which I did. Then I went to see Atticus."

"You shouldn't have opened the door. What if Crawford had beaten me?"

"I don't know. Didn't think about it."

"Go on."

"When I got to Atticus, he didn't seem to be in pain, but when I called him, he couldn't get up. He was weak, but he kept trying. I held his head in my lap. Then you came running, and you passed out, and by then there were several cop cars, and one of the cops carried the dog to his cruiser, and a crowd had gathered, and Debbie James offered to stay with Donna Jo, and I told her Amy was coming, even though I hadn't called her yet, but if she wouldn't mind waiting until then, I'd appreciate it. So I jumped in the car, and the officer called Amy, and we went to the animal hospital."

"Numb Nuts was in our house?"

"Yes."

"How'd you get here?"

"Derek picked me up. He went home about twenty minutes ago. He's very concerned about you. Maybe you can call him."

"I will, in a minute. Tell me exactly what the vet said."

Silence. Somewhere, a clock was ticking. I could almost hear the dripping of the I.V. Then I heard fear, almost tasted fear, as Jessica finally spoke. "He consumed a large quantity of anti-freeze. We don't know how long Crawford had been there. We do know that it was long enough for the poison to take affect, and longer still because of the fight, and waiting for the cops, and the ride to the animal hospital. He started vomiting and shaking. The vet gave him charcoal and I don't know what else. We exchanged phone numbers. He'll call if there's any change."

I didn't respond. I lie there, letting it sink in. I thought Jessica was finished, but she wasn't. "There was a long chain by the kennel, and one those heavy duty pruning shears you use on the branches and things. Any guess what that's about?"

"Not really," I lied. "But I think it was the sound of something metal that woke me. Maybe it was the chain."

"You know, don't you?"

"I don't *know*, but I'm afraid I can guess."

"Well?"

"If you wanted the sickest, cruelest revenge on us, and you couldn't get Donna Jo, you'd kill our dog. Then hang him up by his neck in the kennel, even while the poison was working, so he'd suffer and we'd find him that way in the morning."

"And the shears?"

I cried as I told her, "To collect his tail as a trophy."

Before we could continue, Jessica received a call. It was Amy, who informed us that she had gotten Donna Jo dressed for school and out of the house with no problem. They were going to breakfast, then to school. Jessica thanked Amy, but as she hung up I could tell that new concerns were entering her mind.

"What?"

"The kids. At school. They may have heard things. If they mention things to her, before we get there ..."

"Can you call the school?"

"I've got a better idea, but I may have to leave for awhile."

"That's fine. I'll call Derek and, well, I'm not going anywhere." It had not occurred to me that Derek would be so relieved to hear my voice. As I listened to his concern, and his relief, I once again felt the warmth of friendship replacing the coldness of the previous night.

It was after nine when Jessica returned. She had caught up with Amy and Donna Jo, and after breakfast with the two of them, and while Donna Jo was in the restroom, where she was not resting, Jessica told Amy her fears. Amy had an instant solution. The hospital she worked at often had students come to help out. Granted, none were as young as Donna Jo, but she knew it would be fine. Initially, Jessica wasn't convinced, but Amy insisted and a problem was solved.

It was after noon when the call came. Too much antifreeze, too much time before treatment, too much liver damage. Atticus was no more. No knife wound hurt so much or cut so deep.

It was after two when the I.V. was disconnected, and after four when the doctors reluctantly released me. I insisted I would not be lying in a hospital bed when Donna Jo learned the truth. I made promises to rest, and one tetanus shot and who knows how many stitches later, Jessica drove me home.

It was after six when Donna Jo returned drinking a milkshake from her favorite fast food establishment. She was so excited about all she had seen, and so grateful to her Aunt Amy for a wonderful day. It seemed that much crueler to have to destroy that kind of happiness.

After hugging Amy good-bye, Donna Jo stated, "I need to change my clothes and go see Atticus." That's when the real hell began. Jessica started by telling her that we had sad news, telling her about bad people who do bad things to good people, telling her that sometimes things happen that don't make sense. Then I took over, telling her about my encounter with Frank Crawford. I had covered my bandaged arm with a sweatshirt, but now I showed her. Her eyes widened, and her expression of concern was so pure and genuine that I had to stop talking.

Jessica resumed the tragic tale, explaining the reason for her day with Amy before leading to the terrible conclusion neither of us knew how to express. When she got to the not very grand finale, it was clear that Donna Jo suspected the outcome. "Atticus? Is something wrong with Atticus?"

I finished the chore. Both of us tried to comfort a child who had become inconsolable. She screamed. First she screamed the word no. Then she screamed her dog's name. Then she screamed, "Not Atticus. Not him." Then, the most passive and loving child I know threw her milkshake against the wall and ran into her room, slamming the door.

We found her in the fetal position, staring at the far wall. I lay down next to her, holding her as she sobbed in spasmodic waves; waves that began at the deepest point in her sole and worked their way to the surface, cresting in her heart and overflowing her eyes. I held on, and Jessica sat beside me, rubbing her shoulders and crying with her.

For seven years, Atticus had been our only child. We raised him from puppyhood. He was my first pet. Jessica had grown up with all kinds of animals, but my mother wouldn't allow it, no matter how much I begged. She claimed to have allergies, but I believed then, as I believe now, that she didn't want the hassle, or the dog hairs. Heaven forbid there might be something out of place in our house. So I was a grown man before I experienced the childlike innocence of hugging a dog as his twenty horsepower tail wagged in appreciation.

Donna Jo was sobbing less, but still experiencing the post-traumatic crying disorder that made inhaling a body contorting labor. I was thinking that Atticus was named after my favorite literary character who once said, "It's a sin to kill a mockingbird." I suspect he was right, but if that's a sin, what word is there for murdering a little girl's dog, and her happiness? I was searching for the word when that little girl broke the silence. "Does your arm hurt?"

"A little."

"Were you scared?"

"Yes."

"Were you trying to save Atticus?"

"Yes."

"I'm glad you are home."

"Me too."

"I'm sorry about the milkshake."

"It's okay."

"Atticus never hurt anybody. He was just a big, friendly dog."

"I know."

"It's not fair."

"No. It is not fair."

"This hurts more than the fire."

"I know."

There was a long silence, the three of us lost in our grief. Donna Jo murmured an "I love you," and I answered her, and she repeated it for her mother, and moments later she was asleep, and still I lay there, holding her, loving her, aching for her.

It was dark when we tiptoed out of the room. Jessica was still crying as she cleaned up the mess Donna Jo had made, and I wanted to say there was no use crying over spilled milkshake but it sounded stupid, even in my head, so I didn't. Instead, I tried to sleep, to prepare for the worst day of the rest of our Atticusless lives. The thing about pets is they come into our lives and let us think we're controlling them, then they leave too soon and we learn who was really in control, but by then we're too busy licking our own wounds.

CHAPTER 8

More Aftermath

Or: Heart Screen

Derek was getting ready for another parents' night. This time he was demonstrating what he called a frequent faculty fantasy. It involved consuming enough alcohol to be totally honest and uninhibited with each parent. It consisted of a series of questions, like, "Did you have any smart kids?" or "Were you using drugs during your pregnancy?" or, "Have you considered a parenting course?"

He had witty remarks for all types of parents; the ones whose kids were never wrong, who blamed the teachers for every bad grade, the ones whose child was destined to play in the N.F.L., even though they sat on the bench in high school. There were parents who had given up, and some who never started. There were parents who were overly protective, and some underly-informed.

Derek had often discussed these things, but in the past, I was not a parent. It occurred to me that someday I would have a high school-aged daughter. I found myself listening with greater intensity, a greater sense of urgency.

I guess Jessica was also, because she asked, "What scares you the most?"

It was a serious question, and Derek dropped his stand-up routine. "The drugs. The teen-age pregnancy. The suicides. The cutting."

"Cutting?"

"Yeah, cutting. You're not familiar with it?"

When we shook our heads no, he explained. "Kids will literally cut themselves. They'll use a knife, scissors, a straightened paper clip, anything sharp. They'll make themselves bleed."

"Why?"

"Some do it for attention. Some for self-loathing. Some for the high. Some because it's the one pain they can control. Some because they're addicted."

"Addicted? To cutting?"

"They tell me yes, it is addicting. It's a pain/pleasure thing. It's a release of endorphins, I guess. It starts somewhat harmlessly, if cutting one's self can ever be harmless. It gets out of control. Kids get hospitalized. They need therapy. It's a mess."

"I never knew. My kindergarten students didn't have these problems. I think we may need lots of help as Donna Jo gets older."

"I'll be happy to help, if you need it. But most high school students are fine, and Donna Jo will be, too. Anyway, you have plenty of time. How's she doing these days?"

It was a difficult question to answer. It had almost been a month since Atticus was murdered. Some days were better than others. None of us were ever as happy as we had been, but all of us had our positive moments. Mrs. Larsen said her schoolwork was fine, but she was quiet, even at recess. At home, she didn't exactly mope around, but she wasn't exactly talkative. She painted more, went outside less, read more, played the keyboard less, wrote in her diary more.

Eventually, the conversation turned to Frank Crawford. It was like the scab that everyone had to pick at.

The day after the incident, I started making phone calls. I wanted to know why in the hell Crawford was not locked up somewhere. And I most assuredly wanted to know why I wasn't notified of his release. Theresa agreed that these were good questions, and set out to find the answers. There were none, at least none that made any sense.

Crawford had gone through a two-month rehab. He was out on bail pending his trial. Police Chief Mitchell was not notified of his release. Everyone agreed he should have been, but no one took responsibility for the "communication failure." The chief was irate, and apologized profusely, even though it wasn't his fault. In the weeks that followed, I gave up. I told Theresa, "Everyone's running scared, scared that I might sue them. I'm not suing anybody, but I'd sure like to know exactly whom it is that I should be pissed at. I'd like someone to say, 'Yes, Mr. Donahue, you are right. You and your family were placed in a dangerous situation, and you should have known about Mr. Crawford's release, and I am sorry.' Clearly, that's never going to happen."

Theresa promised that she would always know where he was, but that wasn't comforting. A week after her promise, Frank Crawford hanged himself with his bed sheets in the rehabilitation center that was supposed to be helping him. It made her promise easier to keep. Once again I felt relieved that I had not hit his head when I had the chance. I didn't rejoice at his death, but I didn't grieve either.

It was Amy who suggested the need for a vacation. It was Derek who suggested the place. It was Jessica who suggested the activities. But I was the one who suggested the grand finale.

So we limped on, with a hope and a plan and each other. We shared our vacation plans with Donna Jo, who had never seen the ocean. It was the first time we saw any of the old excitement in her eyes. We set up a big chart with a picture of a white sandy beach. We called it Destination Destin, and we checked off the days until our first family trip.

While we waited, we studied. We read everything we could about protecting Donna Jo's skin from the sun. It really wasn't that difficult. It's too bad there isn't heart screen; some kind of ointment to protect a child from exposure to ultraviolent ways.

CHAPTER 9

The Gift

Or: The Sequel

We began in the Smoky Mountains, taking the path to Klingman's Dome. From there we looked into North Carolina, and Virginia. We would have seen more states if the air had been clearer.

I cannot go to the mountains without feeling their magnificence, and my own mortality. Their majesty moves me, inspires and humbles and thrills me, and I never tire of experiencing their splendor. For Donna Jo, it was her first trip. Her wide-eyed exuberance indicated that we should see to it that it wasn't her last. That was an easy vow to keep.

The Smokies are almost in our backyard, yet we don't visit them frequently. It's as if knowing they are close by is a reason to take them for granted. We can go anytime—so we rarely go. Maybe we'd visit more often if they were farther away. I'm not sure what this says about human nature, but I don't think it's a positive. From the Smoky Mountains we headed South—to white sand and turquoise water and the magic of Destin, Florida.

Every feeling stirred by the mountains is awakened again by the miracle of the ocean. I feel the same awe, the same harmonious blending with nature, the same spirituality. It amazes me that two environments, so different in physical features, can be so alike in their ability to reach into the core of our humanity and awaken that which lies dormant anywhere else. No one had to tell Donna Jo these things. It was like she sensed it, intuitively understood it, like it was the most natural thing to experience. Maybe it is, and she's young enough to just enjoy it, without a need to analyze or verbalize it.

She romped and frolicked and splashed and rolled and laughed and covered her body in a clear briny water and warm sugary sand and relished this brand new gift from an ancient giver of life.

For a week, she was a child again. Even the occasional stares, or the one direct question from a boy who would eventually stomp on her sandcastle, and then apologize at the insistence of his mother, did not change the fact. She was not a burn victim, or a girl mourning her dog. She was a child, enjoying herself and her surroundings and her family. It is no small fete to give some one back her childhood.

It was a glorious week, and a terrible place to leave. I wondered how many firsts we had missed, and how many we might still experience. Donna Jo's first trip to the mountains and the ocean were essential, permanent memories; prerequisites for a life well lived.

I couldn't help but compare my earliest trips to the ocean with that of Donna Jo. She had her family with her, she had a week, and I know she had more fun. I did feel one slight disappointment. Not once during the entire week did I see a jellyfish. By now, our daughter, like most children, had heard her old man's story so often she could recite it herself, but she had never seen the wondrous subject of the story.

We were only a few hours from home, with Donna Jo apparently asleep in the backseat, when Jessica said, "Bear and grin it."

I was not ready, was not really sure what had happened. It had been so long I needed her to repeat herself, which she did with exaggerated exasperation. "Bear and grin it."

The game was on. "Let an umbrella be your smile."

"Don't let your ass hit you in the door."

"Words speak louder than actions."

"A rolling moss gathers no stones."

"Leap before you look."

And then, from the backseat, a small voice said, "A spoon full of medicine helps the sugar go down."

Our stunned silence was followed by laughter. Not just any laughter, this was the, "I can't believe I just heard something that funny" kind of laughter, the lose your breath, hurt your gut, eye-watering laughter that will make you repeat the scenario and laugh just as hard the next twenty times someone brings it up.

Donna Jo waited for her parents to stop being so silly, not exactly sure if she should be laughing with them. She finally got to ask, "Did I do it right?"

We kept laughing while telling her she had done it perfectly. She then asked us to explain the how and why, and a lengthy discussion of the history and the rules and the intricacies of bobble head ping-pong followed. We actually developed the children's version, which Donna Jo planned to introduce to her friends at school.

We were an hour away when Jessica decided it would be wise to let Derek and Amy know we were almost home. It seemed innocuous enough, which was the intent, but an hour later, Derek and Amy were waiting for us when we returned home. Actually, Amy was waiting; Derek was nowhere to be seen. We engaged in the expected greetings, hellos and hugs and how was your trip. It was Donna Jo who asked where Uncle Derek was. It was Amy who told her, "Your mom and dad got you something. Derek has it in the backyard."

Running. Stopping. Yelling. Crying. Grabbing. Hugging. Laughing. It all happened so fast. The golden retriever puppy, the one with the big feet and the hyperactive tail that Jessica and I had selected weeks ago was licking Donna Jo's face, crawling in her lap, jumping and spinning and relishing the attention. Our daughter could not believe what was happening, alternating between asking if this was really her puppy and thanking us for the best present ever.

We stood watching, both couples feeling compelled to hold his or her spouse. No dog would ever take the place of Atticus, but this was going to be a worthy sequel. "What's his name?"

"Actually, it's a her. What's her name? Whatever you want it to be."

"That's going to be hard."

"There is no rush."

Eventually, the adults went inside. It was time to drink the beer and wine Derek had so thoughtfully packed in his cooler. We ordered pizza, and talked about vacations and puppies. Donna Jo and her unnamed companion ate pizza also.

Our friends left early, leaving Jessica and I to handle one predictable problem. Donna Jo wanted the puppy to sleep in her room, and we weren't about to deny her. We had the box and the blankets and chew toy ready. The puppy cried most of the night, but if didn't seem to matter. Our daughter was happy, and all was right with the world.

CHAPTER 10

The Name

Or: The Kid

For awhile, it seemed that finding a name for our puppy was as difficult as finding peace in the Middle East. Donna Jo kept trying. She started with people—Miss Leena, Aunt Amy, Theresa. She didn't like that idea. For a few minutes, I thought she was going to go with Shriner, because of all we had told her about the hospital, but she changed her mind again. Even Charlotte, the magical spider from her favorite story, got her fifteen minutes of puppy-name fame, but it didn't last. I got a little nervous over Jellyfish and Bobble Head, but fortunately, they didn't make the cut.

She was sitting on the front porch, petting a sound asleep golden retriever. I was thinking about the words sound asleep, trying to use synonyms or antonyms for sound, when her sigh stopped the word play. I looked at the Norman Rockwell picture that was living on my porch. She looked up, caught my eye, and in a soft voice, so as not to disturb no name, said, "Tell me how come you called Atticus Atticus."

I gave her the Cliff notes version of my favorite book and my favorite literary character. I told her that I liked the idea on naming my dog after something as special as a powerful, creative idea; a man courageous enough to do what he felt was right, even if others hated him. I told her how I admired what he tried to teach his children.

Donna Jo was intrigued by the word "children." She wanted to know all about them. I knew then what she was going to name her dog. After all, it is

Scout who tells the story, who becomes an outcast in some people's eyes, but who learns never to kill the mockingbirds in our society.

"Do you think Scout is a good name?"

"Yes, but it is more important that you think so."

Her eyebrows almost touched each other as her mental exertion took on a physical countenance. "Scout was good?"

"Yes."

"And she loved Atticus?"

"Yes."

"I know this puppy isn't really Atticus' daughter, but it's kinda like that. I mean, she came after Atticus."

"Well, I guess …"

"Does Atticus die in the book?"

"Do you want me to ruin the ending?"

"No. I can't wait to read it."

"I can't wait either. I hope you like it."

"I will. It sounds like you."

"Donna Jo, that's one of the nicest things anybody has ever said to me."

Her mind was made up, and with the weight of monumental decision-making lifted from her shoulders, she was once again that Destin girl, the one on the beach, the innocent, carefree kid. My mother always hated the word kid. "A kid is a baby goat," she'd huff. She didn't get it. She wanted to talk of children, or little boys and little girls. "Shaw," as they say in the South. "Hell no." Anyone can be a child. A kid takes some doin'. A kid is a child with pizzazz, spunk, gusto. A child is elevator music, a kid is jazz, or rock and roll.

Donna Jo stood up to hug me, waking her new-named puppy. As a kid, she knew that all major decisions should be sealed with a hug. "Thanks dad."

"For what?"

"For the help." Then she knelt down, looking directly into the eyes of her companion. "Hey, Scout. That's your name. Scout. Do you like it?"

Scout answered the only way possible, with a lick on the nose of the questioner. Donna Jo took that as a yes, and the two of them bounded off the porch, heading for the backyard, the woods, and adventures of their own. Maybe they'd find Boo Radley, or at least a little piece of mind.

CHAPTER 11

Pre Storm

Or: Returns

We ended our summer with a reunion that would become a tradition. Once again, Miss Leena and Chief Mitchell would join us. Once again Theresa and Derek and Amy would return. Once again the food and the drink and the conversation would help to bring this unique group closer. Miss Leena and Chief Mitchell, LaMarcus, were also growing closer, as demonstrated by the announcement of their engagement.

Jessica also had an announcement. She was returning to kindergarten; not at her old school, not at Donna Jo's school, but at a new elementary school in Knoxville.

Our life revolved around returning; returning to school, to work, to each other each evening. Our friends would return as often as possible. Occasionally, some of the old problems would return; Donna Jo getting teased about her scars, Jessica coming home upset about a child who was neglected or abused, my periodic recollections of the night Atticus was murdered.

We all had our therapies. For Donna Jo, it was painting, which eventually gave way to a sketch bock, and the keyboard, and Scout. She'd go through periods of intense socialization—sleepovers, movies, roller-skating. Then she'd seem to withdraw, being content with her home and her dog and her solitude.

Jessica also found comfort in art and music, but mostly she found comfort in her family, and in her classroom.

My arm healed, slowly. I had a scar, and stiffness, but I worked to rehabilitate it. My therapy was physical. I worked out more, although most of the time I was inside when I worked out, which is mildly amusing. I also took comfort in planning. I became the vacation planner. As a child, I never went on one vacation that I enjoyed. Sometimes we'd pack up the car and travel long hours to visit some distant relative whose name I barely knew then and don't remember now. We'd spend a few days, I'd be bored and ignored, and we'd travel home. Nonstop, except for my irritating problem of needing to use the toilet. My dad absolutely hated that, unless I could wait until he needed gas.

I think I was trying to make up for that, or, to do my best to give Donna Jo a better childhood. I had traveled some after college, but now, it was becoming my passion. Derek had once speculated, "If all of the kids I teach, the ones who come from bad situations, the ones who hate everyone who is not like them, were somehow allowed to travel, I'd bet I'd have better students."

I thought about that often. If somehow every kid had a chance to see more of his country, and other countries, would we have fewer narrow-minded people? It made sense to me, and I was determined to provide our daughter with the education that comes from traveling. I still had plenty of comp time left, even after using some when Donna Jo was in the hospital. My daughter and wife had identical school schedules, and I was able to match them. We spent a fall break in New England, a spring break in the Grand Canyon, and a week during the summer in San Francisco.

I don't know what I would have done if Donna Jo hadn't loved every opportunity. I was relieved I didn't have to find out. And then we would return, and be reunited with Scout, and our friends, and our jobs.

We also went to the mountains. It was in Cade's Cove that Donna Jo saw her first bear. It was a Sunday morning, and the loop around the cove was surprisingly un-crowded. There were a few cars pulled over, with people pointing and taking pictures. Jessica saw it first. It was a cub, high in a tree. We got out, taking turns with the binoculars; initially unaware that a group of people was heading toward the tree.

It was a statuesque oak tree, alone in a field that was edged by other trees. People were now running across the field, crowding under the tree that held the cub. It was Donna Jo who asked, "Should they be doing that? I mean, we learned in school that wild animals can be dangerous."

Apparently, the adults under the tree had not learned what my fourth grader had. I was wondering if momma bear was around, and said so. The cub was becoming distressed. It wanted to get down, actually started down several times, but the crowd was in the way.

That's when momma appeared, followed by another cub. Momma was pissed, and people scattered as she stormed out of the woods, growling and snapping and rushing toward the tree. Somehow the crowd escaped. We watched as the cub climbed down, and the three went back to the woods. It was a vivid lesson about mob stupidity, one my daughter would long remember.

There were other trips; the chimneys, Laurel Falls, New Found Gap. One crisp fall morning we hiked along the stream that leads to Abrahm Falls. Three river otters decided to entertain us, frolicking and diving and popping up onto the rocks, chasing each other before returning to the water. We watched for almost an hour, and Donna Jo spent the evening drawing remarkable sketches of what she had seen.

Scout grew. We survived a few nights of crying and the ordeal of house breaking, which is a stupid term in my opinion, because nothing in our house got broken. What was broken was the puppy's perception that all of the house is a toilet. I think the house was dog broken, but after that she became a welcome guest in Donna Jo's bedroom. She was not as big as Atticus, and her coat was a little darker, but there were similarities. She was a quick learner.

It was in fifth grade when Donna Jo sat at our dinner table and announced, "I know what my scar looks like." Jessica and I both asked, and she triumphantly replied, "Louisiana."

"Louisiana?"

"Yup. Louisiana. We've been learning our states, and today I looked at Louisiana and well, I asked Melissa, who is now my best friend by the way, and she said, 'Yes, I believe so.' Well, I looked a little longer and I think that's it."

I had to admit, she had a point. She seemed proud of her discovery. That night, I kissed New Orleans and Baton Rouge good night.

Melissa became a fixture at our house. Donna Jo said that she was the only kid in her class who liked bobble head ping-pong, that everyone else thought it was dumb. Melissa immediately gained stature in our eyes, so much so that she joined us on our spring trip to Niagra Falls, and our summer trip to the Rocky Mountains. Our daughter was almost in sixth grade, and for some reason that sounded so much older than the others. She began to care more about what her friends thought, less about what we did. We were on the cusp of puberty and junior high school and teen-age stuff. Stuff is the technical term for all the crap and confusion and chaos that goes into that angst-filled time.

In the summer before her sixth grade year, Donna Jo began asking questions, questions that led to family discussions. What was my birth mother like? Tell me about the fire. How long was I in the hospital? What were my grandparents like? How did Jessica and I meet?

She would go through weeks of questioning, hanging around the house, though not literally, like we were the center of her universe. Then she would drift away, though not literally, and her friends were the center of her universe, and we saw little of her. Then she would return, asking about what we did in high school, or college, or what we were like when we were her age. And then the basic biology questions began, and I surprised myself with how comfortable I was, and I knew this was another of those, "I don't want to be as awkward or as clueless as my parents were" moments. It is also possible that I was thinking about ol' Fingers Costanzo.

Sixth grade was actually fine, except for a few dramatic moments. Melissa found the friendship grass greener somewhere else, causing Donna Jo to say the first cuss word we ever heard her say, although judging by the way she said it she may have practiced. What she said was, "I'm tired of Melissa's two-faced shit." I was semi-impressed.

Donna Jo entered her blue period for a while, drawing darker pictures and playing darker music. I told her it was fine as long as she didn't affect Scout. I told her a bummed-out golden retriever would not be acceptable. She laughed.

Sixth grade was the beginning of Spanish. Jessica and I both enjoyed being forced to brush up on our rusty, not exactly proficient foreign language. That's why Mexico became my latest travel obsession, or L.T.O.

We would actually make the trip, our first to another country and another culture. We saw beauty and poverty, scenic beaches and squalid living conditions, friendly people and dangerous people. We saw Mayan ruins and high rise hotels, and Donna Jo learned what many of Derek's students never would; that there is life and wonder and magic outside of Knoxville, Tennessee.

We would also have the pleasure of sharing in the joy of matrimony. Watching Miss Leena marry LaMarcus Mitchell reminded us of our own vows. It was an honor to be with them on their day.

Sometime, between the summer trip and the annual reunion, I came to terms with three of the scariest words in the English language: Junior High School.

I had an uneasy feeling, a foreboding about it, and I had no reason for it. Maybe it was the fact that I went to junior high school and remembered it for the hell that it was. Whatever the reason, I had been experiencing the elementary calm before the junior high storm, although I was not the one in for the rough ride.

CHAPTER 12

The Storm

Or: Crushes

It was 1999 and Y2K dominated the news. The national news. Our local news, and by local I mean the news at my house, was dominated by The Period. Seventh grade was the year of the period, by the period, and for the period.

First there was the weeping and wailing (and some gnashing of teeth) because our daughter was the only seventh grader in the civilized world who had not had her period. When I rather flippantly mentioned that, with half a century of periods to look forward to, maybe there wasn't a rush. I was greeted with, "What would you know about it?" I was about to answer the question when she stormed out of the room.

Then came the agony and the ecstasy, and my little girl now felt like a woman, and acted like one, at least occasionally. She was a kid one minute, then a woman, then a raging hormonal creature I didn't recognize.

The period was followed by the first crush; at least the first crush on a person Donna Jo might actually talk to, unlike the T.V., movie, rock star crushes of the past. Who decided this emotional chaos should be called a crush? It should only be called a crush when it ends, because that's what it does to your heart. At the beginning, it should be called, "My first insanity." That phrase is far more accurate, and predicts that future insanity will follow.

Donna Jo's first insanity was Jason Lee Lively. Ol' Jason was about the least lively person I ever met. He grunted, avoided eye contact, and walked about as fast as political change in Cuba. For the duration of their relationship, I said all of the right things, which would be absolutely nothing. I was aided by the fact that the duration of their relationship was just over three weeks, which is almost a lifetime commitment in junior high years. All those hearts and initials had to be scratched out, but after two days of mourning, our daughter returned.

Seventh grade was the year Donna Jo hated me. I was no longer funny, no longer important, no longer the person whose opinion mattered. She and Jessica were on speaking terms most days, and on alternate Thursdays they were actually best buddies. I tried not to be jealous, but I wasn't successful. I also tried not to be hurt, and I might have succeeded if it weren't for the vacation we didn't take.

We were to go to Canada. I had done the planning, and I thought we were all excited. Then Melissa re-entered the picture. Apparently, Donna Jo was no longer tired of her shit, because when Melissa's family invited her to go with them to Myrtle Beach, that became the single most important event in the world, and the fact that they were going at the same time we were supposed to go did not matter. I argued for our family time, our tradition, but it didn't matter. I had a choice. I could make her go, and have a miserable time, or I could let her go with Melissa.

Donna Jo went to Myrtle Beach. Jessica and I spent a few days in a chalet in Gatlinburg. It was romantic, and fun, but I still hurt. I was trying to hold onto something that was slipping away.

Three weeks after the trip to Myrtle Beach, Donna Jo got tired of Melissa's shit again. She even got mad enough to confess that the beach hadn't been that much fun, and she should have gone to Canada. I found no consolation there.

Amy rescued my daughter during the summer between the seventh and eighth grade. Jessica had mentioned how bored our daughter was. Amy suggested that she could do volunteer work at the hospital, kind of like a candy striper without the stripes. It saved the summer.

Every morning Jessica drove Donna Jo to Amy's house so they could ride together to the hospital. Every evening Amy drove to our house to drop her off. The last six weeks of the summer were wonderful. Donna Jo loved going to the hospital. She especially loved working with the children. Amy told us that all of the nurses raved about the help she provided. She spent hours drawing. She drew for the children, for herself, and once, in a rare moment of affection, presented me with a picture of Atticus that made me cry. It is a picture I framed, and it now sits on my fireplace mantel, next to Willie Mays.

I actually thought that the bad times were over. I now know it was only the eye of the storm, and that the eye wall often hits the hardest. It would have been a perfect time to write the Great American Novel (hereafter, the G.A.N.). If only I had known.

CHAPTER 13

The Eye Wall

Or: Deep Stuff

The weather during the first three months of school was unusually and unseasonably hot, even by East Tennessee standards. If it hadn't been, things might have been even worse than they were.

The first change affected Jessica. It was her year to be the persona non grata. She and Donna Jo fought about everything—clothes, make-up, curfew, the phase of the moon, the color red, and the direction of the sky. It seemed like the more they fought, the less I did. Occasionally I was the referee, and once or twice I was even the person to confide in.

I did discover one surprising and semi-amusing fact. I am more comfortable discussing sex than my daughter. So is Jessica, and that bothered us. Donna Jo did not know anywhere near as much as she wanted us to believe she did. We knew that by her questions and her reactions to statements. The idea of talking to us clearly made her uneasy. I had hoped that her eighth grade health class would help. I was dreaming. In a just say no, abstinence only climate and culture, the purpose of eighth grade health was to avoid controversy at all costs. I was not surprised to learn that Tennessee ranked fourth in teenage pregnancy, and was about the same in sexually transmitted diseases. So we continued to broach the subject, only to get the facial convulsion and rolling eyeballs that indicated we were only slightly more welcome than terrorists.

I did discover that even the slightest hint about our own sexuality would send Donna Jo into apoplectic shock. "Oh Gross" was like a recurring mantra in our house.

Jessica and I really do continue to have an extraordinary love life. I found myself, as a type of foreplay, whispering, "Hey baby, you want to be gross tonight?" Sometimes, after sex, I'd moan, "Oh gross," softly into my wife's ear. It was important to keep our sense of humor, and our commitment to each other.

The only relationship in Donna Jo's world that remained consistent was the one with Scout. No matter what her mood or who she currently couldn't stand, her dog was always treated well.

I didn't really notice the change. Jessica did. It was subtle, a slight lack of interest here and small lack of appetite there, and only a little more time in her room, alone. The heat wave turned to a drought, and the drought approached record proportions. On one particular Tuesday evening, Jessica asked, "Didn't Donna Jo wear long sleeves yesterday?" Since I wasn't sure what I wore yesterday, I was no help, but I was curious about the question.

"I swear, in this heat, I don't know why she wore long sleeves today. It was like I watched her do it but it didn't even register. Now I'm trying to remember the last time I saw her in short sleeves."

"And you think it means something?"

"I don't know. It just seems odd."

"Of course it's odd. It's junior high school. It's all odd. I think it's supposed to be odd."

"Yeah, well, let's watch this."

We watched. Wednesday morning, in 95-degree heat, our daughter wore long sleeves. She did again on Thursday. By Thursday evening, Jessica had had enough. In a movie, there would have been some theme music playing. *Jaws* comes to mind. She started calmly enough, discussing general things like attitude and appetite, which of course made Donna Jo defensive. Finally, seeing no other choice, she asked, "Why are you wearing long sleeves on these hot days?"

The look of alarm on our daughter's face alarmed us, but her words told us she just liked those clothes better.

Jessica wasn't satisfied. "Are you hiding something?"

"No."

"Then you'll show me your arms?"

"This is crazy. Don't you trust me?"

"I want to. Show me your arms."

"Dad, this is so unfair. You don't think …"

"I think your mother has a reason to be concerned. Show us your arms."

"No."

Her refusal spoke volumes. I told her that, before adding, "It's either a tattoo, a piercing, needle marks, or cutting. Which is it?"

In the silence that followed I found myself wondering which one I should root for, realizing there were no good choices. And still the silence continued. I watched as her demeanor changed, watched as a single tear formed in her left eye and slid down her cheek, crossed Louisiana, rolled down her neck and disappeared under her shirt. I watched as she struggled, and finally willed herself to say, "Cutting," before her face contorted and tears flowed and she rubbed her forehead. "I'm so sorry, I never meant for this to happen, I thought …" She stopped talking, sobbing pitifully.

I saw a little girl, in the hospital, mumbling, "I'm sorry, I'll try harder, I'll be good." I saw more pain than any eighth grader should feel. I saw Jessica sit beside her, and hold her, and tell her that it would be all right. I joined them, holding them both, holding on as I fought the fear that was pounding in my chest.

Jessica whispered, "I need to see," and slowly the sleeve of her left arm unveiled the canvas of the cruel artist. There were old scars, scars that were almost healed. There were new scars, scars that looked raw and painful, ready to spew the precious red liquid with the slightest touch of cold, sharp steel. The right arm was slightly better, or less grotesque. There were three well-healed lines on the back of her left leg, just below the knee. I felt every mark, every scar, as if it were being etched on my heart.

"I never thought … I mean … I never wanted … I'm so sorry, and, and, I'm scared."

"Can you talk about when and why, and … well, can you help your mom and me understand?"

"I think it started with the dreams, the bad dreams."

"What bad dreams?"

"The ones about fire. I wake up sweating, afraid, struggling to breathe."

"Why didn't you tell us?"

"I don't know. I was afraid. Afraid you'd think I was weak, or crazy."

"We wouldn't."

"Yeah. Anyway, I'm not doin' so well in school. I'm not sleeping. I heard some kids talkin' about it, I tried it, I hated it, it freaked me out, but I tried it again, and I hated it less and it didn't freak me out, and well, it just kinda happened. I thought I could stop anytime, but I guess I never wanted to stop. It felt, I don't know how to say it, it felt surprisingly good, even though it hurt. And I was in control, and it was my ritual, my escape, my, my freedom."

"Is there freedom if you are no longer in control?"

"No. I never meant to hurt you two. You've got to believe me. You must hate me."

Both of us answered. We answered with promises, with words and actions, with assurances or our undying, unconditional love. We answered with a plan to address the problem.

It was not a good night for sleeping. We explored our own sense of guilt, our own hurt, and our own fears. I wondered what would have happened if Derek had not mentioned the problem some time ago. Jessica wondered what would have happened if the weather had turned cold.

The next day we both left work early. We met Donna Jo's guidance counselor, who could not have been less helpful. She said, "Yes, I think it's a serious problem, especially with our girls." She gave no insight into the problem or what to do about it. If she had said, "Yeah, shit happens," it would have been as helpful.

Donna Jo's teachers weren't much better. We wanted them to know so they could watch our daughter, so they could help us if they observed anything that seemed odd. They all said they would. They all seemed indifferent. I left feeling like I had just sentenced my daughter to being viewed as a weirdo in their eyes. I began to understand why Donna Jo might be doing poorly with this dream team. I told her that. I asked her to do her best and not worry about her grades. I told her we'd get tutors if she needed it. I told her we'd get her help for the cutting, and I begged her, "Please. No more. No more cutting. No more scars."

She promised to try. Help came from Amy and Derek. Their understanding and non-judgmental nature helped us. Their friend, a Dr. Stanley Brewer, was a therapist who worked with patients at the hospital where Amy worked and the school where Derek taught. He agreed to work with our daughter, who initially hated the idea, but grew to accept and even appreciate the help.

Our daughter was returning; returning to the happy person we were used to. Just when we were ready to declare victory, something happened to remind us about premature celebrations.

No one at Donna Jo's school knew she was seeing a therapist. We all wanted that to be the case. It would have remained that way were it not for the guidance counselor. She had scheduled individual meetings to help students select classes for the following year. It was a redundant exercise, since the high school counselors would do the actual registration with everyone later, but she was doing it anyway. To expedite the matter, students went to see her in groups of ten. She'd give them general instructions, then talk to each one in her office. When Donna Jo went for her individual conference, there were four or five other students in the outer office waiting for their turn. She would tell us later that her counselor never closed the door. That she began by asking, "Aren't you the one with the cutting problem?" Donna Jo never said a word, just nodded and looked toward the door. Then she was asked if she was getting help, and when she nodded yes, her counselor told her how great that was. When she asked if she had any scheduling problems, she shook her head no and left.

She left the inner office to the sound of hushed laughter. She left the outer office to more giggles, less hushed. And that was all it took. For the rest of the school year, she was called psycho. Her peers would point, they'd laugh, they'd cough, "Psycho" as she passed. Some even reenacted the shower scene from the movie, something we had to explain to her when she asked about it.

It was cruel. I wrote the strongest letter I have ever written to that cow's ass of a counselor, with a copy to the principal. I got profuse apologies, which were meaningless, and promises that Donna Jo would not be ridiculed, which was bullshit. All they were doing was covering their ass so I wouldn't sue, which I wasn't going to anyway.

Help came from a surprising source. Our neighbor, ol' Junior, son of Numb Nuts, for reasons unknown, had begun talking to our daughter. Kenny had grown; he was a six-foot tall eighth grader. He had been shaving for some time. We secretly suspected that he was in his twenties, but we couldn't prove it. One day, Kenny heard the cruel comments directed at Donna Jo, and he went ballistic. That stopped most of the teasing. The irony of that action, especially after our initial meeting, was not lost on Jessica and me. We even felt guilty about the "Numb Nuts and Junior" comments.

Eighth grade was the perfect grade for yet another cruel rite of passage. Donna Jo was to experience the dreaded "B" word. Braces. It was a perfectly horrible ending to a perfectly horrible year. We knew the summer would have to get better.

CHAPTER 14

The Best Laid Plans

Or: STSS

Donna Jo looked forward to high school, if for no other reason than the fact that it wasn't junior high school. I wasn't so sure. Her school, not that she actually owned it, was one of those schools fed by several junior highs. I like the word fed, or feeder schools, it made them sound like piranhas, or vultures, or carnivores. Different feeder schools meant the possibility of a new start with new friends. It also meant that she would attend one of those high school factories—a massive, sprawling plant with three thousand students. It sounded like an easy place to get lost.

Derek knew teachers at that school, and he found out what classes to take, which teachers to take, and who to stay away from. It was a monumental help.

Amy was able to arrange for Donna Jo to work at the hospital again, this time for a small amount of money. Although our daughter almost never smiled thanks to the braces, she did seem happier. In fact, she actually looked forward to resuming family vacations after a one-year hiatus. We planned to go north to Maine and Canada. It was not to be.

A week before the trip, Donna Jo was accidentally scratched by a child she was helping. The little boy was raising his arms so she could change his hospital gown. His thumbnail scratched her, "Right in the middle of Louisiana," as she described it. It was a cut, nothing more. Because she tended to wear her hair long and straight for scar concealment purposes, it was hardly noticeable.

All of us, including Donna Jo, had forgotten about it by the day before we were to leave for Maine.

When Donna Jo told us she felt weak, we thought she was just tired. When she said she felt nauseous, we thought it was something she ate. When she said she felt dizzy, we took her to the emergency room of the hospital where she worked. By then, her blood pressure was dangerously low.

She was immediately admitted, and once again we watched our daughter become weaker as I.V.s were started and blood tests were administered. Donna Jo's color was a scary shade of white, and her temperature continued to rise. She perspired as she lie there, unresponsive, looking for all the world like an older version of the child I saw for the first time in Cincinnati, minus the burns. It seemed like just yesterday, and yet a thousand years ago, when my heart first ached from that hopeless hospital feeling. Fear and uncertainty are never more prominent, more dominant, than they are at the bedside of an unresponsive child.

We learned a new term: Streptococcal Toxic Shock Syndrome: STSS. Although it is usually associated with tampons, in this case it began with an infection, a skin infection; a skin infection from a small cut on the cheek. To this day I don't know if Donna Jo's scarred skin contributed to the condition, although I doubt it. I may have asked. I may have received an answer. I don't know. I do know that I went from hoping to take a vacation with my daughter to hoping that I would still have a daughter.

Fortunately, this was not going to be a lengthy stay like we had experienced before. Once the right combination of medicines was found, Donna Jo recovered quickly. We had serious concerns about her kidneys and liver, but she would be fine. It took some time to get her energy back, but most of her recovery was done at home, with the help of Scout.

Donna Jo was substantially improved when the doorbell rang one Sunday afternoon. I opened the door and almost didn't recognize the nervous woman standing there. Her hair was different, and she wore better clothes, cleaner clothes. Arlene Crawford was asking if she could speak to me.

I invited her in, curious about her purpose. She was equally curious about where we lived, or at least our life style. After scanning the room, she began, "I heard 'bout Donna Jo. I have a friend who works at the hospital, in admissions. She told me. I wanted to know if she was all right."

She could have called to find that out, so I suspected there was more, but I told her about Donna Jo's recovery as Jessica walked into the room.

"Kin I tell you somethin', somethin' 'bout my husband and me?"

I wanted to say no, that I wasn't interested, but that seemed a bit excessive and cruel, so I invited her to sit down.

"I understand if you hate me. I know we was wrong in many ways. I'm glad you got her. Couldn't say that when Frank was alive. I woulda, well, I'm glad you got her's all."

I realized I was watching an act of courage. I wondered why she had chosen this particular time, and I suspected she would tell me if I were patient.

"I wanted you to know that Frank warn't always a bad man. When we first met, he was so sweet and kind to me. Wouldn't never harm me. Then he changed, not all at once, more gradual, you might say. He got all messed up on drugs, and it was like I didn't know him. He scared me. I told him Donna Jo would be better off with you'ns, but he wouldn't hear of it. Anyway, I just wanted to say I'm sorry 'bout the past, and I'm glad she's okay."

She stood up to leave. I looked at Jessica, who gave a slight nod to the question my eyes had asked her. "Would you like to talk to Donna Jo?"

"No, I don't think she'd want to know me, not after all you must have told her."

"You'd be surprised how little we have talked about it. It's okay, in fact, I think she'd like it."

"If y'all think it would be fine, well, I'd sure like to see her."

Jessica excused herself and went to get Donna Jo. I felt slightly awkward waiting for them to return. Arlene broke the silence. "I'm still working at the convenience store, but I'm takin' night classes. I'm tryin' to get my medical assistance license. I'd like to help people."

I was thinking about her last sentence when my wife and daughter returned. I've know hundreds of people who can't bring themselves to apologize about the simplest things, who are embarrassed at the slightest hint of a family problem, who run away from problems. Arlene Crawford wasn't afraid to apologize. We all know she'd been dominated and abused by her husband. Yet here she was, facing her past and still talking about helping others.

We left the room. We felt it was important for Donna Jo to talk to her real aunt, without interference from us. We did hear Arlene say, "My what a beauty you have growed up to be. Lord, how you have changed."

They weren't together long. We asked Arlene to stay for dinner, but she refused. She expressed her gratitude, told us how proud we must be, and left.

I didn't know how Donna Jo would react. She said it felt weird. We had a long talk about her past and her relatives. We promised her that she never had to speak with her aunt again. We were pleasantly surprised when she said, "I don't know. It was weird, but it wasn't a bad weird. It's the only real family I've got." Then, when she saw our hurt faces, she added, "That's not what I meant. You are my real family. I just meant, uh, I meant ..."

"Biological family?"

"Yeah. Biological. Sounds creepy when you say it that way."

We finished the summer without incident. It was time for high school.

CHAPTER 15

Freshman Year

Or: First Base

"If I tell you guys something, will you promise not to freak?"

My wife's eyes told me that I would be the official spokesperson for this one. "Do we usually freak?"

"Actually, no. You're pretty cool that way. But this is a little different."

I was tempted to tell her that asking me not to freak about something she thought would make me freak was a good way to make me freak. I didn't. It would have been freakin' ridiculous. Instead, I promised that we would do our best to be freakless.

"First, look at my arms." Donna Jo was wearing short sleeves. Only the faintest traces of her self-abusive past could be seen. "I haven't cut myself since that night we talked. And I won't."

That was not freak worthy, although it was wonderful news, and we told her so. We knew more was coming.

"Can I tell you why I won't cut myself?"

"Of course."

"Because I don't want to kill myself anymore."

I heard our pendulum clock ticking. I heard some insect fly into our picture window. I heard the fluorescent light bulb. I heard my throat clear, and I heard myself breathe, "Tell me."

"I wasn't just cutting myself. I tried a few pills. I smoked some grass, three times to be exact. I'd wait until you were asleep. I'd sneak out. Don't ask where I got it. It doesn't matter. I just hated myself. I … I just didn't want to live."

"Can you tell us why?"

"Because I was tired. Tired of being scar face. Tired of being laughed at. Tired of being ugly, of not having a boyfriend. Tired of school."

"What could, or should we have done?"

"You saved my life. Again. You confronted me, I got help, I'm fine. Actually, that's not the entire truth. This summer, when I was in the hospital, I thought I was really going to die and I didn't want to. I thought of Miss Leena, Aunt Amy and Uncle Derek. I thought about the little boy who scratched me. I even thought about Scout. And I realized I hadn't even read *To Kill a Mockingbird* yet, and I knew that … well, I knew that you loved me, and you went through hell to get me, and I don't know why I didn't think of that before, but I did when I was lying in the hospital bed. So I'm telling you this now so you will know that you can trust me. So you know that I am grateful, and that I love you."

My moist eyes told Jessica that she was now the official spokesperson. Through her own tears, she spoke of our unconditional love, and our willingness to listen. She walked her to our mirror, and pointed out Donna Jo's glimmering eyes. She told her that her smile out shown any fading scar, even with her braces. She told her to look, really look at herself; to look at the entire reflection. "I can't make you see the beauty that I see, but I can ask you to accept what you see, and to trust me when I tell you that you are beautiful."

Donna Jo promised to try. She also told us one final item. "I made a promise that I won't do drugs. I also made a promise that I will always keep my promises."

I didn't ask whom she made those promises to, but in the spirit of full disclosure, she told us. After an emotional reminder about her past, Donna Jo promised Arlene Crawford that she would learn from her parents. The second promise she made to herself.

The next morning, my daughter went to high school. We only thought we were prepared.

We went one entire, blissful, uneventful week. No anger, no tears, no teasing. We almost went a second week, but Thursday morning I received a call from the school secretary. My daughter was in violation of the dress code.

As I drove to the school I tried to remember what she had worn. I also remembered all those days I had arrived at school wearing something different than what I had on when I left the house. If my mother ever knew …

I found the assistant principal's office. Donna Jo was wearing a skirt that seemed vaguely familiar. In fact, it was a skirt she and her mother had purchased two weeks earlier. It turns out that the skirt actually ended above the knee. Barely. But that was enough, because rules are rules and too short is too short and we need to get off on the right foot (as opposed to the left one) and we are trying to set a tone (cue the elevator music) and everyone hoped I'd understand. I didn't, and I said so, politely. I mentioned the class time that was being missed, but I obediently took my daughter home so that she could dress more appropriately. On the way out, I passed three people wearing shorter skirts than my daughter's. One was a teacher.

Donna Jo returned in jeans. She stayed out of trouble until the following Tuesday, when once again her parents were guilty of allowing their daughter to dress inappropriately. This time it was her pullover top that was deemed offensive.

The top was long-sleeved. There was no shoulder titillation here. The fabric was solid, thick enough to avoid the titillation caused by sheerness. It had a mock turtleneck collar. There was no plunging neckline, no cleavage. Unfortunately, it was form-fitted around the stomach, and relatively short. In other words, it was in style, and this particular style allowed the top to barely touch the top of her jeans. It really wasn't a problem, except Donna Jo made the mistake of putting a book on top of her locker while she emptied her backpack. She reached for the book at the same time her favorite assistant principal came around the corner. Stretching for the book had caused her top to ride up, exposing a bare midriff, and dare I say it, a belly button. Right there in broad daylight, in the middle of the school day.

No amount of protest, no demonstration that showed her top clearly covered those offensive body parts when she wasn't stretching mattered. Rules are rules, and a belly button is a belly button, and I got to visit the school again. I reminded the assistant principal of some of the issues that existed in his school, some of the ones Derek complained about in his own school. I indicated my surprise at the priority of my daughter's navel was given. I'm sure this administrator wanted to give me detention. He couldn't, but he could and did assign it to my daughter. It was, after all, her second offense. The next violation would be a suspension.

For the rest of the semester, Donna Jo was very careful about her clothing. She avoided trouble when the cold weather arrived, when everyone wore safe, bulky, non-offensive clothing.

Aside from the fashion-Nazi, school actually went well. She made new friends, enjoyed most of her classes, and explored various school clubs and activities. She was more pleasant at home, and there was never a doubt in my mind that she was keeping her promise to Arlene Crawford, and to herself.

Donna Jo made it until March before she was "bad" again. This time it was Harry Potter's fault.

My daughter hadn't really been caught up in the original Pottermania. She decided she wanted to see what that excitement was about. Two days before the spring break recess, her friend Vanessa brought the first two volumes to school. I mean this friend of my daughter blatantly carried not one but two books into the science class they shared. She proceeded to actually place the books on my daughter's desk. They were not wrapped in plain brown paper. They were visible to anyone who wanted to see them, and one person who did not. Mr. Brian "Intelligent Design is Pure Science" Sheffield was not the least bit happy to have such demonic filth in his classroom, and did not mind saying so. Loudly. In front of the entire class.

Fortunately, most of the class knew that he was a nut case. Vanessa felt terrible about her friend being treated to poorly, and told Mr. Sheffield what had happened. Then she became the brunt of the tirade.

Once again, I found myself writing a letter, with a copy to the principal, expressing outrage over the actions of an educator. I was assured, by the principal, that my daughter had a right to read what she wanted. I wanted to write back, "Thank you so much for generously allowing the constitution to exist," but I didn't. What I wanted was for her to be free of the harangue of a cow's ass like Sheffield, but I knew that was asking a lot. I told Donna Jo about Derek's experience with *The Color Purple*. She immediately phoned him so they could share stories. She also mentioned that Mr. Brian "Charles Darwin is the anti-Christ" Sheffield had perfect initials.

At the end of her freshman year, Donna Jo made what would turn out to be one of the most significant decisions of her life. She decided to take the school's journalism class during her sophomore year. She also decided that she had waited long enough. This was the summer she would read *To Kill a Mocking-bird*.

CHAPTER 16

Sophomore

Or: Second Base

Donna Jo spent the summer working with Aunt Amy at the hospital for minimum wage, except for the two weeks we spent in Maine and Canada. She successfully avoided sharp fingernails, and we had successfully vacationed together. Finally.

She also read. She read the third Harry Potter book, *Cyrano de Bergerac,* and *The Phantom of the Opera.* The Broadway cast of the *Phantom* came to Knoxville, and the three of us sat spellbound by the power of the music of the night.

We talked about her reading. I loved watching and listening to my daughter as each new literary experience bombarded her head with previously unthought concepts, unfelt emotions, unheard insights. But nothing compared with Our Book.

We discussed *To Kill a Mockingbird* chapter by chapter. She loved Atticus, and understood why I had used his name for my dog. She loved Scout, and was more pleased than ever that she had used her name for her dog. But most of all, she loved Boo Radley. Her eyes glistened with just the right mixture of animation and moisture as she talked about his plight as one of society's mockingbirds. I could tell that, in spite of all she had been through, she still felt uncomfortable with her scars. I longed for the wisdom of Atticus, for that knack of saying exactly the right word at the right time.

Atticus wasn't really needed. My daughter would find her own way. She'd begin with a new set of teachers; teachers who weren't afraid to try new things.

Teachers who actually pushed and encouraged and celebrated success. Success became the expectation, and the expectation became the reality.

Donna Jo jumped on the rite of passage carousel, and by the time it was over, I felt older, and not the least bit wiser. It began in October, with the removal of her braces. In November, she got her learner's permit, as in Jessica and I could take turns enjoying the adrenalin rush of being in a moving vehicle that may or may not be under the control of the driver. That same month we got to experience the first "serious" boyfriend, not to be confused with the lively crushes of years past.

I think it is a law, or perhaps a commandment, something along the lines of, "Thou shall experience, at least once, your daughter dating someone you absolutely can not stand." By February, Donna Jo could not stand him either. It took her that long to realize what her old man knew from the start. Paul Dunning was not very bright, not very polite, and not very friendly. That did not stop him from being part of the first real kiss rite of passage, nor the arriving home an hour after you are suppose to be home rite of passage. Those were the two we knew about. By the time she came to her senses, she had purchased her first Christmas present for someone outside of the family, and spent her first New Year's Eve away form home.

In March, The Big One happened. My daughter received this magical three and a quarter inches by two inches, laminated key to freedom. She was a licensed driver. Her world could not be better. Mine could not be scarier.

Parental hell is watching your child leave your driveway in your car for the first time. And the second time. And who knows how many times after that. Parental heaven is hearing your safe child drive up your driveway with your car still in one piece. Hell and heaven became part of our daily life.

Through boys and cars, making out and breaking up, school stresses and excesses, Donna Jo thrived. She made it through an entire year without a dress code violation, and she made it through an entire year without being called scar face, or psycho, or a satanic worshipper of Harry Potter. Friends visited, music blared, and the phone, the infernal, peace-killing, mind altering phone was busier than Jerry Falwell at a Tele-Tubby convention. Donna Jo was getting her wish. She was becoming normal, at least, what she viewed as normal. By the time the carousel slowed for the summer, the period of normalcy was also winding down. Sometime later, Donna Jo would observe, "Normalcy is overrated."

CHAPTER 17

Junior

Or: Third Base

Donna Jo cut her hair. Actually, she paid a professional to cut it, and I'm not talking a little trim. It was a bold move, one I understood perfectly.

Since the fire, my daughter had worn her hair long, in an attempt to make her scars less obvious. Now her hair barely covered her ears. There would be no attempt to mask anything. I thought she looked great.

We had a long weekend at Virginia Beach, where several jellyfish were discovered and avoided. We had an earlier than usual reunion with the usual suspects, then we said good-bye to our daughter for two weeks. Donna Jo was spending the last two weeks of her summer break at newspaper camp.

By the end of her sophomore year, Donna Jo had fallen in love with journalism. The teacher and advisor for the school paper was Ms. Diana McFarlon, a young, vivacious woman with a keen sense of humor and a love for writing. She became the topic of conversation on those increasingly rare occasions when we actually ate dinner together. For the most of the semester, Donna Jo learned how to write, how to research, how to edit. It wasn't until the last month that she actually had something published in the paper under her name. It was a small article about an upcoming choral performance, but it was enough. Donna Jo was hooked, and in the last issue of the year, she had a much larger piece about graduation. She immediately began a scrapbook, promising to fill it by graduation.

Her school newspaper was impressive, far superior to any I had ever seen. They published every other week, and the students were free to write about any issue they wanted. The only demand was that it be factually accurate and objective. The editor, almost always a senior, had his own column, where he or she would give editorial opinions. It was a cherished and honored position, and Donna Jo's holy grail.

The journalism camp was in North Carolina, and we received daily updates from our aspiring reporter who attended it. To say that she loved the camp is to call a sunset pretty, or a snowfall white. She returned absolutely energized, and would remain so, no matter how many people and events tried to change that.

Donna Jo made it through her sophomore year without a dress code violation. She didn't last a week the following year. This time the fashion crime was—a drum-roll please—the cursed spaghetti strap.

Spaghetti straps were strictly forbidden. I think they showed too much shoulder, and we all know what too much shoulder leads to. Even during the hot weather, most of her classes were cold because of the air conditioner, so Donna Jo had put on the dastardly garment to wear before and after school, and a long sleeve shirt to wear in school. It was a good plan except for her chemistry lab, where, while concentrating on her experiment in a warm lab, Donna Jo lost her head and removed her shirt. Ten minutes later her favorite assistant principal entered the room, looking for another student. His dress code radar immediately focused on her, and she was removed from class. She was able to convince him that it was an accident, that she would put her shirt back on, and the republic would once again be safe, but she did receive a stern lecture about rules and attitude.

Later that day, there was a fight in the hall between two males. The following morning, two females went at it. She would learn, through her investigative reporting, that it was rare to go an entire week without a fight. She also witnessed boys pushing and intimidating their girlfriends, and occasionally girlfriends striking boyfriends, yet her spaghetti straps and other dress code issues seemed to receive more attention. In fact, the dress code was discussed more often than drugs, violence, cutting, eating disorders, college choices, or teen pregnancy. She knew she had a story.

Ms. McFarlon let her pursue it. She had to interview the administration and quote them accurately and extensively.

The day the story ran, Donna Jo received many compliments from her peers. Her English teacher also complimented her. Her history teacher didn't. In fact, he ridiculed her in front of the class, and then told her to be quiet.

When she refused, she was sent to the office where she received a two-day suspension for being insubordinate. I knew my daughter was going to be fine when she insisted that I say nothing on her behalf. This was her problem, and she would handle it.

The next issue contained several letters to the editor about the issue, including a lengthy and critical response signed by the administration. It was only the beginning.

I think Ms. McFarlon liked the way Donna Jo handled the criticism. I'd bet that she saw some of herself in my daughter, and that's why she pushed her, coached her, and trusted her. It was as if fate had brought them together, and it was as if fate was going to force the action. When Aaron Jones, the senior editor of the paper, came down with mono, there really was only one logical replacement. Aaron would miss a lot of school, he would have a lot of work to make up, and he would ultimately decide he just wasn't up to returning to his position. It was Donna Jo's, and it would remain hers until she graduated.

Her first op. ed. piece was about censorship in general and the Harry Potter version in particular. She ruffled a few feathers, which would make sense if she was writing for ducks and chickens, but that's what people said she did. Nothing too serious, although several letters from concerned Christians were received and printed in the next issue. Her real trouble began when she decried gay bashing. That's when she lost friends. That's when her history teacher, who had been civil if not friendly after the first incident, refused to even acknowledge her. Her "A" average suddenly disappeared. She was thankful for the "C" he grudgingly gave her.

After a welcome hiatus, the taunts and cruel comments returned. She heard scar face occasionally. Psycho made a short-lived return, but suddenly, as if some community consensus had been reached, she became Fag Lady, or Lesbo. Her locker was vandalized. She got prank calls at night, some just gross, others threatening violence.

We talked nightly, the three of us. My heart broke when she talked about her treatment, but it mended and swelled with pride when she talked about her determination to continue. She was Atticus Finch fighting unpopular causes, Don Quixote tilting at windmills.

She did receive some support. Ms. McFarlon, who took her share of criticism for allowing "such trash to be printed," never once wavered in her support. A number of students told her that they respected her and agreed with her. Those conversations were always in private.

Not every column was controversial. She wrote about things taking place in the school and community that she thought were positive. She wrote about the dangers of meth and actually received praise from the principal. During those times, the criticism slowed, but then she'd take on a social issue, like sex education in school, and she'd take a pounding. She was sure of one thing. People were reading her work.

It would have made perfect sense for the junior prom to be held without Donna Jo there, which I suppose is why she ended up going. That and a young man confident enough to go with the biggest social outcast in the school.

Donna Jo pretended to be annoyed by all the fuss—but we could tell she was secretly happy, and perhaps relieved. I learned a great deal in the process. I learned that modern day proms cost more than my first car (a beat up Pinto). I learned that guys think getting ready for a prom requires about fifteen minutes longer than getting ready for any other event, while girls think getting ready for the prom requires more planning than D-Day. I learned that seeing your daughter in her first formal gown is like seeing a rock concert and a sunset and a snow covered mountain at the same time. We said all of the typical things about her beauty and our pride, her growing up and our growing old. I managed to wait until the pictures had been taken and the wonderful couple had left, but I had my emotional moment.

When it was over, and we were having the "tell us all about it moment," Donna Jo said the prom was a "C." She liked being dressed up, at least for a while. She liked the music and the dancing, but when the thrill wore off it was still high school drama playing dress-up. There were numerous post-prom activities, most of which consisted of drinking, with occasional vomiting. The good news was that her date wasn't into that. The bad news was that he believed that the payoff for the prom meant intercourse. Donna Jo was not about to become a cliché. That's when the date ended.

Once again, I found myself marveling at the poise and courage of my daughter. I wished her prom had been better, but I'm still glad she had the opportunity. I wished her junior year had been less painful, but I'm glad she stood her ground. I realized something else. We only had one more year together, one more year of seeing each other on a daily basis before college became a reality. I worried about that.

CHAPTER 18

Bobble Heads

Or: Ruin That Tune

"There's a good moon risin'."

"Are you serving?"

"Do you have to ask? There's a good moon risin'."

My guess was song titles, with a word changed, but I wasn't sure. I couldn't think of anything else. She served Credence, I returned The Stones. "White sugar, how come you dance so good?"

"Lucy in the sky with pearls."

"Devil with an orange dress on."

Jessica didn't respond, at least not immediately. The tears came first. "I'm sorry. You win. This is a stupid category and I … I thought this would help. It hasn't."

I knew what was wrong, and it had nothing to do with our game. It had everything to do with the day and the present we were giving.

Not once had our daughter hounded us for her own vehicle, even though most of her classmates drove. We'd been secretly shopping, and recently purchased a used Honda Civic. It was at Derek's house. Tomorrow, the first day of her senior year, was to be the grand presentation. Jessica was excited about the gift, but depressed by its symbolism. For this kindergarten teacher, senior year was going to be emotional hell.

"I thought you were crying about the devil with the orange dress, orange dress, orange dress, devil with the orange dress on." It was my best Mitch Ryder imitation, which is to say it sounded nothing like him, but it made her smile. Making Jessica smile may be my most significant contribution to our marriage.

"I've got to stop this. If I'm this teary-eyed now, what's May going to be like?"

"I'll visit you."

"You'll what?"

"I'll visit you, in the institution."

Her smile was widening. "Which institution might that be?"

"I believe that would be the Benign Institution for Teachers Considered Hopeless. That would be ..."

"I get the acronym."

"I thought you would. But it's BITCH, because I just wanted to say it anyway."

"Are you calling me a bitch?"

"No. Never. I'm just referring to the situation. And trying to be funny."

"Yeah, well, keep trying."

"Thanks. Jessica, we made it through her burns, the court cases, her educational setbacks, her cutting, her being picked on. Come to think of it, those things happened to her. I know we suffered too, but if the three of us can survive all that, we can certainly survive her senior year. Besides, growth and graduation and college—those are good things."

"I know. It's just that ..."

"It's just that you love her, and you're so damn proud of her, and you'll miss her."

"Yes."

"Me too."

"You're a good dad. And a good husband."

"Yes. I am. And I'm funny as hell. You should remember that."

"Adam?"

"Yeah?"

"Hell isn't funny."

"How do you know?"

As planned, the car was waiting in the driveway. Donna Jo thought that I was going to give her a ride to school. When we were both ready to leave, I said, "Listen, there is a car in the driveway that's blocking mine. Why don't you move it for me?"

She had no idea what I was talking about. "What's a car doing in our drive-way?"

"Not much of anything, really. Just kinda sittin' there. Why don't you move it?"

"Whose is it?"

"Well, I guess it could be yours."

That's when the screaming and the hugging and the running started. Followed by the touching and the admiring and the starting. And the thanking. And more hugging and thanking. I suspected that very few students had a better first day of school. Jessica returned to being an emotional wreck as Donna Jo drove off to begin her final year of high school. I joined her.

CHAPTER 19

Senior

Or: Home Run

High school is a time for hate. We join cliques to protect ourselves from the hatred of others, only to then hate those who we thought might have hated us. Hate unto others as they would hate unto us, a survival of the hatest.

We hate those who look different, who dress different. We hate because of race, color, sexual orientation, and religious affiliation. We need people to tear down. This year is no exception. We have found a new target. Even though they make up less than three percent of the state's population, and even though there is not one student in our school who belongs to this group, I hear consistent vilification of these people. This year's object of racist venom is the Mexican. You'd think the Bible belt would be better than this.

Thus began the first editorial of Donna Jo's last year. I know how she felt. I recently hired a worker of Mexican background. He was, and is, the best worker I have. I immediately had to fire someone who had been there for more than a year. Seems that deep thinker didn't understand why I would hire, "one of them." I asked if he meant a male, hoping he'd think about his stupidity, but he said, "No, a darkie." I told him he had five minutes to leave.

Derek was having the same problem. His students made ethnic slurs, told racist jokes, and complained about all the jobs "they" were taking from white people. Derek asked the class to name one person who had lost such a job, and they couldn't, but they decided to never let the facts get in the way of good misconception, and continued to perpetuate the myth, and the hatred.

Donna Jo was guilty of a "take no prisoners" approach to journalism. Still. It was partly because of her background and her passion. But her senior year was markedly different. Some of her classmates actually agreed with her, and found the courage to say so.

Senior year. Two words that speak volumes. The message to the senior is different than the message to the parents, yet somehow they all understand one significant truth. This is the beginning of the end of life as we know it. Change is coming and comfort zones are going, as are whatever remnants of childhood innocence might have remained. Charles Dickens wasn't writing about senior year when he talked about the best of times and the worst of times, but he could have been.

Donna Jo had the worst of it. Filling out college applications and scholarship forms was a full-time job. So was going to school. So was the newspaper. Our sleep-deprived daughter was not always pleasant. It became mathematical in proportion: $A^2 (B^2 + C^2) = BFM$. A^2 represents Donna Jo's grumpiness, and $B^2 + C^2$ equals Jessica's reaction to A^2 plus my reaction which equaled a Big Freakin' Mess. It would last until Thanksgiving, when the applications were finished and Uncle Derek set us all straight on what we were experiencing.

Then things changed. The change was slight, gradual, subtle. Donna Jo was home more often, sometimes just hanging around for no apparent reason. She spent less time on the phone, more time with Scout, less time in her room, more time in the kitchen, or the living room, or any place Jessica and I happened to be.

There seemed to be a change in her writing as well. While she continued to write about the controversial issues of the day, the war in Iraq, abortion, environmental issues, she became more interested in less weighty issues. She wrote a sarcastically funny article about cell phone addition (C.P.A.), suggesting that it was only a matter of time before her generation pierced their ears to make cell phone earrings, and pierced the corner of their mouth with a stud that held the mouthpiece when the phone was opened. When the conversation was done, the phone would be snapped shut and worn like a large earring. She wrote about the ring tones, and what it said about a person's personality, even suggesting a contest to find the perfect tone for various celebrities, or teachers. The paper was deluged with "suggestions," many of which were humorous in a vicious sort of way.

She wrote about her generation's preoccupation with tattoos and body piercings. She found irony in the fact that some wanted to intentionally change what their skin looked like, yet made fun of those whose skin was changed by forces beyond their control. She discovered the power of parody, the beauty of irony, and the wisdom of witty sarcasm. She used them all, yet somehow seemed less antagonistic, more refined, more sophisticated.

Sometime between Thanksgiving and Christmas I arrived home to a mildly surprising and amusing event. Jessica greeted me with, "Donna Jo has asked someone to eat with us."

"Who?"

"Do you remember Melissa?"

For a moment I didn't. Then, my less than steel trap of a mind went way back to the archives to retrieve, "You mean eighth grade Melissa, who broke Donna Jo's heart?"

"That's the one."

"What ..."

"I don't know."

I would not have recognized the attractive, mature young woman who joined us for dinner. Or was it supper? I never really know which is better to use. Melissa was initially quiet, seemingly shy. Then she warmed up, at least that's what most would call it, although her temperature stayed the same. We talked about generic, safe topics, and she could not have been more pleasant. When she left, Donna Jo told us what we both wanted to know but were afraid to ask.

"Melissa is in my history class. It's the first class we've had together since freshman year. Two days ago, she asked if we could talk. I was surprised, since, well, you know what happened. Anyway, she told me how sorry she was about how we weren't friends anymore. She said she respected me, wished she'd been more like me, especially with her reputation."

I knew Donna Jo wanted me to ask. So I did.

She sighed, hesitating, as if she were debating how blunt she needed to be. "She's known as being easy. They call her whore, or ho, slut, tramp."

She let those words hang in the air, like the final notes of a piece of music, although there was nothing musical about them. She waited just the right amount of time, then continued, "She's had it worse than I have. All because she had sex with a big mouth jerk with the sensitivity of a jellyfish." She obviously hadn't planned that analogy. She glanced at me with a smile. "Okay, maybe the sensitivity of a cactus. I didn't mean to bring up your past. What happened was, during her sophomore year, Melissa thought she were pregnant. She wasn't, her period was just unusually late, but she was in a panic. By the time she found out she wasn't, the damage had been done. Her jerk had started rumors, first that she was pregnant, then that she had an abortion. And here's what gets me. The mentality of our school is that while she is a slut, he's just a good ol' boy.

"For a while, she lived up to the label. She drank, she did drugs, and she had sex. She figured, 'What the hell, the damage has been done.' Only she wasn't happy. She changed, cleaned up her act, tried to start over. Only in high school, you can't start over. There is no forgiving. She does less of the sex, drugs, rock and roll scene than most of the people who call her names, yet somehow they're still considered pure, and she's a ho."

I could tell that an editorial was forming in her mind. I could also tell that she had forgiven Melissa, had forgotten the past hurt. I admired that. Melissa would become her closest friend, and a frequent visitor at our house.

December 31, 2003. Donna Jo went to Melissa's house. My wife and I ate our traditional seafood dinner, built a fire in the fireplace, sipped champagne, and had our traditionally quiet romantic evening. It was shortly after midnight when I went outside. I stood in the brisk night air, staring at what I was reasonably sure was Pleiades. I had started the day in the year 2003. Now it was a year later—the year of my daughter's graduation. I found myself being pulled by two opposing forces. The first was lunar in nature, as if I were the ocean, and I was being swept back into a tidal wave of the past. Memories of Frank Crawford and Dr. Thakkurian and Davis Richardson III flooded my brain. The opposing force was solar in nature, as if I were a planet being pulled along, orbiting the future. Graduation and college and uncertainty dominated the elliptical path. I don't know why I stood there. It just seemed like the place to be, like maybe a shooting star would give me something to wish upon, or some other celestial revelation would magically appear.

Jessica and Scout appeared instead, and I suppose there was a certain magic in that. We just stood, looking at the stars. Well, the humans were. I think Scout was looking for food. Sometimes just standing in natural beauty and silence is enough. It's like I never know exactly what I'm looking for, but I always seem to find it.

It was early March when The Letter arrived. Vanderbilt University was pleased to accept Donna Jo Donahue for admission. I was not surprised. Her grades and tests scores were excellent. Her essays, which I only got to read after she had sent them, were extraordinary. Her teacher recommendations were wonderful. When I read what Ms. McFarlon had written about her, I cried. Then I made a copy and framed it. No, I wasn't surprised she was accepted, just happy, relieved, and proud. The pure, unbridled joy Donna Jo exhibited after reading her acceptance letter, the hugs and kisses, the instant, "We need to go somewhere special for dinner," the repeated chorus of, "We are so proud of you," and the refrain of, "I can't believe I got in," all those things created a classic lyrical composition. It was a ballad, one that said, "It has all been worth it; all of the pain, the scars, the teasing, all of it, each and every heartbreak, has been worth it."

CHAPTER 20

Graduation

Or: Grand Slam

This is my last editorial. I thought I would use this space, a space that I have been privileged to occupy for a year-and-a-half, to thank those who have impacted my life.

To those teachers and administrators who cared more about clothes and appearance than what I learned, I say thank you. You taught me about priorities.

To those teachers who cared—who pushed me, who made a difference, I am truly grateful. I will thank you individually, but I did want to say that you taught me your subjects, but you also taught me to love and value learning.

To those students who made fun of me, who called me scar face and psycho and lesbo, I say thank you. You taught me about grace under pressure, and how to treat people.

To my friend Melissa, I say welcome back. You taught me to value time, and to forgive.

Everyone needs a mentor. I had the best. Ms. Diana McFarlon believed in me. I owe her my sanity. She taught me the power of following your dream. That's exactly what I'm going to do.

Thank you Theresa, Leena and LaMarcus Mitchell, Aunt Amy and Uncle Derek. You became my family, and you taught me to value and treasure those people who love you.

Thank you Aunt Arlene Crawford. You taught me about human dignity.

Dad. I have come to love your twisted sense of humor, your stories, and your willingness to listen. You gave me Atticus and Scout, and faith to do what I thought was right, even if it was unpopular. I love you.

Mom. You were my first teacher, and my best one. My earliest memory is waking up in a hospital room, and seeing your face. You taught me about unconditional love, and that is why and how I love you.

To all of my readers: I tried my best. I hope it made us think and grow. It was never meant to be personal. Thanks for reading.

Arlene Crawford attended graduation, then, after much cajoling, she joined Theresa and the Mitchells and the Pearsons at our house to honor Donna Jo and Melissa. And our neighbor, Kenny James, and his mother, Debbie James attended. I had vowed to give up derogatory nicknames, and I was truly happy our neighbors joined us.

That happiness lasted until Debbie decided that this festive occasion was the time to bring up that terrible night when Frank Crawford attacked me. With Arlene becoming mortified, Debbie launched into a replay of the event, concluding with, "I swear, it was plum crazy, the derndest thing I ever seen. Wouldn't expect no white boy to be so loco, less'n he was doped up."

Donna Jo went to where Arlene was sitting, put her arm around her, and introduced her to our storytelling neighbor. At least Debbie had enough sense to be embarrassed. A short time later, at the urging of her son, who made it clear he needed to leave this lame party and get to "somethin' happenin'," I watched them leave. My ban on nicknames was revoked. Numb Nuts and Junior would always be Numb Nuts and Junior.

I watched with pride as two high school graduates, young women who had seen the ugly side of high school, left for a quiet evening, away from the parties of their peers. They were going to visit Ms. McFarlon, and then they were going to a late movie and a later dinner, celebrating not only their graduation, but the joy of finding each other—and themselves.

I let Arlene know how much I respected her, and how much people like Numb Nuts don't matter in the overall scheme of things. I let each of our friends know how much I valued them. When they had all gone home, and my wife had gone to bed, I found myself wide awake, as opposed to being narrow awake. I found myself staring at a picture of Atticus. I grabbed the thirty-three inch, thirty-two ounce Willie Mays and a bottle of beer. I cordially invited Scout to join me on my front porch.

Willie still felt sleek and smooth in my hands. I set the beer down and swung the bat, slowly. It was one of those movements that somehow connected me to my childhood, and to the immortals of the game. I swung faster, relishing the way the bat cut through the air with a swishing sound. I took my stance, waited for the pitch, swung for the fences. In my mind, it was another homerun, number 342,499. Give or take. I wondered what Scout was thinking.

I sat down on the top porch step, the barrel of the bat resting on the step below, the handle forming a perfect platform around which to wrap my hands. I rested my chin on my hands as Scout snuggled closer. I thought about every cliché I had ever heard about how fast time moves, and agreed with every one of them. I had once worried about being too old to adopt a daughter. In some ways I felt younger now than I had thirteen years ago, which made no sense at all, except that maybe Donna Jo had kept me thinking young. Maybe seeing the world through her young eyes was enough. Maybe we become young by the company we keep.

Once again I found myself alone on my front porch, drinking a beer and contemplating the stars. Of course I wasn't really alone. Willie Mays and Scout were with me.

Graduation. It's a pretty cool word. It meant far more to me as a parent than it did when I was a graduate. Not *The Graduate*, like Dustin Hoffman. Just A Graduate. Donna Jo may have walked across the stage and gotten the magic piece of paper, but Jessica and I graduated also. We were about to enter postgraduate parenting. I knew we were ready.

CHAPTER 21

Full Circle

Or: The Bobble Head Legacy

It all began with a dream. Julianne Moore was kissing me and whispering into my ear. Only the kissing became so real that I opened my eyes. Julianne was gone, but Jessica was laughing and hugging and kissing me. "Were you dreaming?"

"Maybe."

"Julianne?"

"Maybe."

"You want your dream to come true?"

"Okay, but ..."

"I know. I'll wait."

When I finished the pre-foreplay routine, I returned to bed, where we made quiet love. Quiet love is what you learn to do when you are afraid of waking your child.

We finished the quiet session, and I lay on my back, Jessica resting her head on my chest. "Our daughter goes to college today."

"Yeah. I know."

"What do you think?"

"I think it's wonderful."

"Me too."

"And I think that Julianne doesn't hold a candle to you."

"Nice touch."

It was true. No fantasy can take the place of the love of your life. A moment later we heard Donna Jo's alarm clock, and moving day was about to begin.

Jessica hurried to get dressed. I lay there, letting my mind wander. I never did write the Great American Novel, (here after the G.A.N.). At least not yet. Maybe I never will. If I do, I hope it somehow contains all that I've learned since Donna Jo entered my life.

I've learned that people who worry about accents and geography are gawd awful bores, ya'll. I've learned that there is a little bobble head in all of us; that it's okay to get in touch with your inner bobble, just so long as it's not a steady diet. I've learned that teachers and nurses touch and save lives, and that five-year-old burn victims have more courage than most of the things our society labels as courageous. I've learned that a fictional character like Atticus Finch is still real and inspirational almost half a century after he was created, and that unlike old soldiers, old dogs neither die nor do they fade away, at least in our memories. I've learned to hold on to Willie Mays and let go of old fears, especially those about parenting. I've learned that picking up an occasional jellyfish isn't all bad; in fact, it's a small price to pay. Afterall, there is a lesson there, if you can learn it, a story, if you can tell it, and humor, if you can find it. But most of all, I've learned that we all have scars, but they don't define us. How we got our scars is not as important as how we react to them. Donna Jo taught me that. She is one hell of a teacher, just like her mother.

978-0-595-43110-6
0-595-43110-0